VENDETTA

ISBN: 978-1-945532-17-7

Published by:
Opportune Independent Publishing Company
Cover Art Designer: *Helen Ackles*
Stock Photo: Neonshot ©123RF.com
Editor: *Anita Bunkley*
Printed in the United States of America

For permission requests, write to the publisher,
addressed "Attention: Permissions Coordinator," at:
info@opportunepublishing.com
www.opportunepublishing.com

Author available at www.angelicarroberts.com

Acknowledgments

God is truly good! All thanks first goes to my Heavenly Father who gifted me with the talent, love and desire to write.

At an early age I was introduced to books by four great people. My dad forced me to read classic novels (yes, forced)! My late mother would always read and leaf through lifestyle magazine articles with me. My Grandma Bracey bought me all the children's books that had a black face on the cover (ALL of them); and my Aunt Helen kept me up-to-date with all the best fiction novels. Thank you all for pouring words into my life, it is because of each of you that I write today.

I am grateful to my entire family, amazing friends, sorority sisters and FAMUly who continue to share in my appreciation and thirst for a pen and paper. I seriously have the best group of loved ones and supporters. All of your encouragement has meant the world to me. This book is just as much yours, as it is mine.

Special thanks to my test readers, financial supporters and mentors for investing time and energy into my craft and into VENDETTA. None of this could have been possible without you.

Jasmine Furr, thank you so much for joining this project and for sharing your poetry and advice with me. Your motivation and knowledge helped me more than you know.

Thank you to my editor, Anita Bunkley, for helping to make sure my first novel would be a great one!

Thanks to all of the staff at Opportune Publishing Co., Shanley McCray, you have been a true blessing.

Last but certainly not least, I would like to thank all of my readers who are helping me by spreading the word! Please keep in touch by submitting reviews, leaving comments and sharing emails:
Info@angelicarroberts.com
Instagram.com/read.write.roberts,
Facebook.com/angelicarroberts

With Love,

Angelica R. Roberts

PROLOGUE

The Beginning (Maya)

As Chaka Khan's song Sweet Thing rang throughout the apartment, I watched as Mama swayed to the beat of the music and fried some mouth-watering chicken. This was her Friday specialty. The crackling of the chicken grease mixed with the smell of sweet cornbread, macaroni and cheese, plus her homemade lemonade always made my stomach grumble with excitement. As I looked on, Mama kept singing the verses the best way she knew how. Though she was a bit off-key, she certainly knew all the words.

"Love me now or I'll go crazy!" she belted out as she used the spatula she was stirring the lemonade with, as her microphone. *"Ohhhhh Sweet thaaaang..."* Turning the fake mic to me, on cue, I grabbed it and continued the song for her, "Don't ya knowww you're my everyyythang!"

Although I was only seven, Mama played music so much around the house that I started to pick up on all the latest songs. Smiling, she rolled up the sleeves of her tattered velour robe, and reached down to kiss me on my forehead. "You will always be my everything, baby." Facing back to the counter, she continued to stir the mixture in the pitcher. As she bopped her long bushy fro up and down to the music, I chose this time to sneak into her bedroom and play dress-up in her clothes. She was in a good mood so I knew she wouldn't mind. While she continued to sing, I sprayed her new Angel perfume on my young neck. *Hmm, this isn't enough.* I thought about my Aunt Deborah and how we could always smell her a mile away, as Mama would say. I wasn't sure if that was a good thing or not, because Auntie Deb kind of stank to me. Before I could consider this for much longer, I heard a loud pounding on our front door.

"Open up Kendra, I know you're in there!" yelled a familiar voice.

Suddenly I heard feet shuffling, and the music in the kitchen was silenced. Looking through the cracks of the door, I saw Mama run into my brother's room. Before I knew it, she flew out from there with him in her arms. Spotting me peeking around the corner, she urgently whispered, "Come on girl!"

I didn't know what was going on, but the look on Mama's face told me I better follow her instructions, and to the T.

"Ok Mommy," I whimpered back in fear.

As she grabbed my hand, the pounding on

the door intensified. I was led to the window overlooking our apartment complex. Before we could open it and hop out, the door suddenly burst open and I noticed my daddy on the other side. He was holding a gun, and had a crazy look on his face. Stumbling wildly through the doorway, he headed straight for Mama. After Mama dropped my one-year-old brother from her arms, then screamed for us to run, my father began beating my mama's face with his fist. I knew this wasn't right; my pre-k teacher Mrs. Jefferson always taught my class that a boy wasn't supposed to hit a girl. Before I could react, a loud bang-bang noise rang throughout the apartment, and I watched as Mama slumped to the floor, holding the side of her head. After Daddy was done with her, he pointed the gun towards Junior.

Placing myself between my brother and the gun, I shielded him with my little arms, hoping it would be enough to protect him. I was the big sister so I knew, since Mama was hurt, that I would have to take care of Junior. Finally, more shots rang out. For a second I thought I was dead. After touching myself in various places and realizing that I wasn't hurt, I looked up and saw my daddy laid out across the entrance of the apartment. He had shot himself.

Looking over at Mama, I realized she was no longer holding her head. Instead, she lay still, in a pool of blood, with her eyes wide open. In a daze, I rocked Junior and myself back and forth until help came. Less than an hour later, police officers and the paramedics showed up, thanks to our elderly neighbor Ms. Francis, who had overheard the exchange. It wasn't until they arrived that I noticed Junior, who had been sick with a fever over the last few days, had thrown up all over my dress. Looking down, I saw that he was shaking wildly and barely breathing. This wasn't the first time he had shaken like that, and I heard mama once explain that his condition was called, having seizures. The medical team grabbed him out of my arms, strapped him onto along white bed, which Ms. Francis called a stretcher, and rushed him out of the building.

Gently taking my hand, Ms. Francis wiped my tears, held me, and then took me along as she followed the ambulance in her car to the hospital. The entire way, I asked her what was going to happen to my brother. After promising me that everything would be okay, we arrived at the hospital ten minutes later. Soon after getting there, the doctor announced that Junior was dead. That day, I lost all the family I knew. Under the care of my neighbor, Ms. Francis, that night I knew my life had changed forever.

Lost and Found
by Jasmine Furr

Sometimes we are found when we are lost
Inside ourselves
Sometimes we tell the world
Don't Search for me
Don't look for me to find me where
I thought was all I had
But I didn't
He will say
I just found you
And sometimes
In the middle of nowhere
Somewhere
Inside this stranger
Is me
And in his eyes of lost placement
I find a piece of me
We find each other
We find family
Inside each other
And ourselves
And right then we know
That love will never leave us alone
In family we always have a home

PART I

CHAPTER 1

We Like to Party (Maya)

In a crowded upscale establishment in Washington, D.C., two friends and I enjoyed a night out on the town. Club 14th Street was on fire. Bodies covered the dance floor and go-go dancers danced on platforms in every direction. The laser lights gave the venue an electric feel and the music blaring through the speakers helped to liven up every partygoer's good time. It was obvious the club owners were trying to mirror the nightlife scene in New York City with the theatrics and exclusivity that the club seemed to provide. In order to get into VIP, one must not only have the money to spend, but the connections and looks to match it. Luckily, we had all three, plus some.

"Ya'll this is my song!" I yelled over the music.

Together, we stood up and danced behind a glass wall on the third floor, where bottles were popping and food was being served. We were separated from the rest of the scene happening below but were still as live and energetic. Snapping my fingers and dancing to a mix of Marvin Gaye's song Sexual Healing, I silently thanked my girls for dragging me out of the house for a night of fun. Almost as if she were reading my mind, Ivey, my best friend, smiled.

"See! I told you it would be a good time. You haven't been out in months. It's your birthday weekend, there's no way I was letting you stay home tonight."

With a smile, I playfully swatted her arm and shared a grateful look with my small group of girlfriends. If it weren't for Ivey and Taylor, I would definitely be at home preparing for my big case that was fast approaching. Back in the day it was normal to see me club hopping and on the scene, but the older I got the more I just wanted to focus on my career. These days I was more about work than play, which according to my hefty bank account was just fine. I was the youngest attorney and one of the few black women at my prestigious law firm and I fought everyday to be taken seriously by my colleagues.

As a defense attorney in the nation's capital, I was responsible for helping alleged criminals. In short, it was a career that I took very seriously. Besides arguing important cases in the courtroom, I made television appearances, spent time in the community with my sorority sisters, and attended networking events and galas with other young professionals. The only reason why I came out tonight was because it was my 29th birthday.

Great, I thought to myself for the millionth time, only one more year until I'm thirty. Leaning against the glass wall, my thoughts were interrupted when a cute Hispanic girl walked by our section, accidentally bumping into Taylor. In true Taye fashion, she launched right into attack mode.

"Watch where the hell you're going," Taye said, rolling her eyes. "You stepped on my shoes."

Looking nervous, the poor woman tried to apologize, but gave up when she saw the evil glare in Taye's eyes. I grabbed my friend's arm to calm her down as the tall and curvy chick who had been on the receiving end of Taye's mug, moved out of harm's way and walked to the very end of the section.

Taylor, or Taye as we most often called her, was the loud-mouthed, fashionable, and Blasian beauty from Philly who could talk her way out of any situation. We met a few years ago when I hired her to help me find a condo. As a real estate agent, she was a city slicker who could talk a good game. Unfortunately, outside of work, her good girl persona often took on an edge and she would come across to some as a beautiful girl with a bad attitude. With a Korean mother and African-American father, sometimes her behavior made her appear to be a bit stuck up and extra, but she really wasn't. The girl was just pretty convincing, which helped her a lot when it came to selling high-priced properties.

"Calm down, it was an accident," I said in her ear. "Leave it alone."

"You yapping ass females are ruining my vibe," snapped Ivey, who was clearly annoyed. "I'm going to find our waitress so we can get more drinks."

That was Ivey, of course, always wanting to continue on with the party. With her bubbly personality and soft demeanor, she was the epitome of a party girl; but having been raised in D.C., she also had a sharp edge to her. After connecting in high school, over a decade ago, we became inseparable. Not only did we grow up attached at the hip, but we also decided to attend the same historically black college, right in the heart of the city. Our careers were totally different and very time consuming but we both managed to make time for one other. As a full-time radio personality and freelance journalist, she was a bit nosy, but her nosiness always landed her major stories. Her portfolio boasted entertainment, sports and news articles, and even interviews with prominent people like First Lady Michelle Obama, Rihanna, and LeBron James. She was living out her dream and doing it well. It also didn't hurt that Taylor and I always knew the gossip before it hit newsstands. She was our connection into the best clubs, exclusive events, and to celebrities.

Closing my eyes, I continued moving my shoulders to DJ Kris's mix and started to feel the effects of my D'usse. Before I could get back into the sound, the Deejay brought the tempo up in the club with TLC No Scrubs. I stopped my groove when I noticed Taylor jump up and look at every single man in the vicinity, screaming about how all of them were scrubs. Pointing her well-manicured index finger with no shame, she popped her booty and looked up to the sky, as if to ask God why men were even on this Earth. Unwanted attention was being brought our way. Women passing by giggled, and men looked on while shaking their heads. I was beyond embarrassed. This girl's man issues were the worst, but they stemmed from her father who'd been locked up for the majority of her life.

A sharp nudge pierced my side, taking my attention away from my bitter best friend. Ivey dug into me as our waitress, who walked up behind her, held out a bottle of Ace of Spades Champagne. Finally taking her hands off of me, Ivey's eyes pointed me to the entrance of the club. Moving away from the glass, I took a seat and waited for her to explain the excitement. Ivey's intensity took Taylor's attention away from the song and she sat down next to us, wanting to know what was going on.

"Maya, look who just walked up in," Ivey squealed.

It was a little after midnight, but it seemed like the energy of the club picked up just a little bit more as a few members of the Washington Cougars NBA team made their entrance into the club.

"Why are ya'll staring so hard?" Taye asked with an attitude. "Ivey, you got us looking like a bunch of groupies."

"Girl, shut your lonely ass up. You need to be the main one in here checking for these dudes." Brushing her Chinese styled bangs out of her eyes, Ivey leaned forward to finish addressing Taylor.

"If you had a man, maybe you wouldn't be so damn over-the-top and mean. And just so you know, I don't want one of those little ball players; I want a meeting with their new star power forward, Damien Roseland. He just got traded to the Washington Cougars from New York, and rumor has it, he fell out with the owner of his former team. No one has had a chance to snag an interview with him yet, he hates the media, and I want the exclusive 4-1-1. I'm not seeing him in the crowd here, though."

Taylor looked like she wanted to say something smart, but decided against it. There were very few times that anyone could get her to shut up. This seemed to be one of them. Before the night was over, Ivey made sure to make eye contact with one of the players seated in the booth across from us. Taking a drink from my glass, I looked up and noticed his friend trying to get my attention. After sending a small smile his way, I continued on with my night. Drumming my fingers against my leg, for a second, I thought about how cute the guy was. Whoever he was, I wasn't interested, though, and I didn't care how fine he was. I was too busy with work, plus my dating history wasn't exactly the best.

For the next thirty minutes, we trekked downstairs to the actual dance floor and got lost in the music and the crowd. Ivey and Taylor threw it back while I did my customary two-step. I was by no means a dancer, and always kept it safe with a simple move and a slight backside jiggle. The guys around us didn't seem to mind, and I caught several looks from attractive men of all shades and sizes.

Once the rowdy crowd started pushing and stepping on toes, Taylor grabbed our hands and led us back to the table to order some food. Almost as soon as we sat down, I rubbed my eyes, feeling them become heavy. It was only 1:00 a.m. but like I said, I couldn't hang like I used to. The next day was Sunday, and even though it was the weekend, I had to meet up with one of my clients to iron out the details for my upcoming trial. This meant that I had to get home and sleep off my liquor in the next couple of hours. *As soon as I eat this pasta, I'm out of here*, I thought after placing my order.

"Hey ladies," said a deep New York accent,

interrupting my thoughts. Following the direction of the voice, I noticed it belonged to the guy who had been flirting with me earlier. With Patron in his right hand, he confidently smiled at the table full of beautiful women and set the bottle down in front of us.

"Mind if my friend and I join you?"

Inside, I groaned. I wasn't up for talking to this man or to anyone else. Before I could dismiss him, I saw Ivey beam with joy. At that moment, I knew that it was too late to say anything, so I decided to keep my mouth shut. No one wants to be looked at as the cock blocker of the group, right?

"My name is Vince, and this is Chris," he continued while stretching his arm out to shake each of our hands and to get our names. When he got to me, I, surprisingly, felt a tingly sensation run up my arm as he held on to me and caressed the top of my hand. Finally, I snatched it back and displayed the phoniest smile of the night. "Nice to meet you, I'm Maya."

Soon after introductions were made, our food arrived. With the arrival of our new guests, I figured it would be best if I just headed home.

"Looks good," I said to our waitress. "Can you just bring me my check please? They can share my pasta."

Wearing an apologetic smile, I told my girls and our visitors that I had to be up early. My friends knew about my big trial coming up, so they didn't put up a fight. Plus they had the attention of some sexy basketball stars.

"Hell no, it's your birthday you're not paying for anything," Taye insisted.

"Birthday?" Vince joined. "Well none of you ladies should be paying then. Can you put this on my tab? I was just sitting over there. "When he pointed to the area where members of the team were gathered, the waitress looked confused.

"That's fine with us," Taylor hurried to say. With a quick nod, the younger waitress rushed back towards the kitchen. Typical Taylor, I thought, she took anything that was free or on the house, even though she had her own money to spend.

"Wow, thank you for this," I said. Without acknowledging my appreciation, Vince simply smiled back and said, "Happy birthday."

Before I could stand up and leave, a line of scantily clad bottle girls walked towards our table holding four bottles with sparks flying out of them. A birthday song blasted from the speakers, and all I heard was, "Go shawty, it's your birthday…"At that point, I realized my crew had set me up. Enjoying the attention, I sat back in my seat and decided to enjoy just one more glass of the good stuff. Conversation was easy and I felt myself loosening up around Vince, who somehow stayed in my face for the next hour. Determined to make my exit, I hugged my crew and was finally out.

Walking through the crowded club was a

hassle. My liquor had worn off and I was starting to feel sleepy and agitated. Once I reached the exit to the club, I felt a tug on my arm. To no surprise, it was Vince.

Pushing through the door, he continued to follow me into the late night spring air. For a second I considered ignoring him, but finally decided to hear him out. Tilting my head slightly, as I sometimes did whenever I was appraising someone, I faced Vince with my piercing stare and waited for him to say something.

"Um, I would love to keep in contact. Can I get your information before you leave?"

For the first time all night, I realized just how sexy this six-foot-five man was. With short wavy hair, an athletic frame, straight white teeth, and the cutest dimple ever, I couldn't help but feel weak at the knees. Despite how fine this man was, I decided to suppress those thoughts.

"I don't give out my number. If you find it, feel free to call."

Knowing that he wouldn't really put up the effort to look for me, I strutted to the town car that was waiting for me right near the exit. As my driver sped off down the boulevard, I made a point to ignore a stunned Vince who remained outside the club.

"*Oh yeah, she'll be mine,*" he whispered to himself.

CHAPTER 2

We're Coming Out (Damien)

Pulling up to the party, I knew tonight was going to be wild. Janet and I had been dating for almost a year, on the low of course, since neither one of us was too fond of the paparazzi or any attention outside of our careers. Unlike so many women I'd been with before, Janet had her own. She was successful, wealthy, and probably the most genuine woman I'd ever met. Every time we were together we laughed and had fun. We hadn't been intimate yet and that was the best part. She was a lady, and to me, that made her the total package. Tonight was the first time we decided to be seen together in public, and later she said she had big plans for us. To say I was a little nervous would be an understatement.

Not only was I labeled a ladies' man, but I was also only twenty-three-years-old. In my eyes, I was young, but Janet, who was four years older than I was, had a way of making me feel like I was ready for something serious. In all my years, she was the only person who truly seemed to get me. My phone vibrated and the smoothest voice I'd ever heard came over the line.

"Baby where are you? My party started an hour ago."

Everything in New Jersey/New York lasted for hours, so in my head I was right on time. Smiling at her obvious desire to see me, I let her know I would be inside in ten minutes. Shortly after hanging up, my agent, Vincent James, pulled up behind me. Handing our keys to the valet, we walked into Janet's New Jersey digs, ready to have a good time.

"How was D.C. man?" I asked while dapping up my agent of three years. He had gone down there the previous weekend to check out the scene before I officially moved to D.C. to join my new team.

"Good, business as usual. I think you'll have a smooth transition when you get there. I hung out with some of your teammates and I have a good feeling about them. I also met this cool chick named Ivey who is a pretty thorough journalist and radio personality. She's interested in an interview. I want to look more into her background but I think she could be a great person for you to do your first interview with since leaving the Knights. I'll keep you updated."

Digesting this information, Vince looked at me out the corner of his eye, waiting for my response. He knew better than anyone how much I hated talking to the media. Sensing my uncertainty, he dropped the conversation altogether as we approached the party. Almost as soon as we walked in, the crowd of guests acknowledged me. After speaking to a few people, I decided to leave Vince and search for Janet. Noticing her talking to Richard Harding, one of the most talented film directors in the game, I gently walked up behind her and slid my arms around her waist. Not even surprised, she grasped my hold and leaned back into my chest. Remembering her manners, she stood up straight and began introductions.

"Richard, please let me introduce you to Damien Roseland."

"Mr. Harding, it is a pleasure meeting you," I began. "I'm a fan of your work. Side Stepping is one of my favorite movies of all time."

Beaming at the recognition, Richard shook my hand. The look of appreciation in his eyes was unmistakable and I could sense that Mr. Harding was looking at me with a little too much interest.

"Well, Damien, I'm a fan of yours as well. Not of your new team, but definitely of you as a player," he jokingly said. With no offense taken, I smiled back with gratitude. Richard excused himself, planning to mix and mingle with the rest of the crowd, leaving Janet and me alone. However, before leaving, he made sure to graze the side of my arm with the tip of his finger, after making sure Janet wasn't looking. It was then that I realized the big-time director was gay. In no way am I a homophobe, but I hated when gay men would get too close and test me. "Baby I think he's going to put me in his next movie," my girl said in a hushed, yet excited voice.

Raising my eyebrows, I knew that would be a huge deal for her career and that it would be best to keep my personal opinions of the man to myself. She had done just fine so far, but was still waiting for her breakout role to help progress her career. She had ambitions of being the next Angela Bassett or Cicely Tyson. She wanted diverse roles, including drama, suspense, and action, and I knew she would get there. Reaching to move a tendril of hair that had fallen in her eye, a light bulb flashed in the distance. Remembering that we weren't alone tonight, unlike how we'd been for the past year, I grabbed her into a tight embrace and just held her. This woman was amazing. A couple of hours went by until I finally had my girl all to myself.

CHAPTER 3

Art of Seduction (Damien)

"Ms. Springer," I whispered huskily into her ear. "Will you be mine tonight?"

All the guests had departed and the real party was just starting. After taking my hand, Janet led me into her master bedroom where a night of pleasure awaited us. Placing her earrings on the nightstand, she proceeded to shed her Roberto Cavalli cocktail dress and unpinned her high bun. I watched in excitement as her light brown shoulder length hair cascaded around her shoulders in soft waves. Following her lead, my Armani slacks and dress shirt ended up next to her pile as I guided her into the bed.

Smiling shyly, she whispered, "I thought I was already yours."

Watching her lick her lips caused my penis to jump. My big man was ready for some action. It had been so long and I was beyond hungry. Laying Janet down softly, I marveled at how smooth and radiant her caramel complexion was. With her petite five-foot and 125-pound frame, she only took up about a quarter of the huge bed and she looked absolutely stunning. After looking at her for a few minutes, I walked to the wall to adjust the switch and dim the lights. Finally, it was time for me to satisfy my appetite. Gliding back to the bed, I grabbed a condom off her massive dresser and slipped it on. Naturally, I'm a selfish lover, but this girl who was laid out before me did something to me that made me want to give her the world. Seeing her anticipation, I slipped to my knees and sent her into a fit of ecstasy as I slowly moved my tongue in and out of her warmth. Her juices laced my tongue, giving me a taste of something sweet. Moaning for more, I knew that it was officially show time. Spreading her thighs, I handled her with the care that I knew she would appreciate. I was a big guy and this was our first time together, so I wanted to be careful not to hurt her.

"Baby, you have five seconds to put that thing in me."

Her words snapped me out of my lovemaking. During our sexual exploration, I quickly learned that Janet was a fireball and liked it rough. Picking her up, I tossed her over and entered her roughly from the back. Her pleasure moans made me go faster. Several positions and an hour or so later our adventures were over. After cuddling for about 30 minutes, I knew I had to go. The next day

I had to be in Washington for a special welcome celebration that my new team was throwing for me. Standing up from the bed, I kissed a sleeping Janet on her forehead and moved towards the door. Looking back once more at my sleeping beauty I made a promise to make her my wife, one day soon. Quietly walking to the front door, I paused for a second in the foyer. Something seemed a little off. Shaking off the thoughts, I locked the door on my way out with my spare key and headed home to finish packing.

CHAPTER 4

The Dream (Maya)

He was handsome, but that was not what caught my attention; he seemed so familiar. I stopped mid-stride to observe him reading a book on the front lawn near the courthouse. For a second I forgot where I was, until a nudge to my side made me jump.

"Let's go. Stop trying to flirt with that guy. If you're not going to speak, then keep walking. We're already running late."

Glancing once more at the man with the ebony skin, big eyes, and low haircut, I turned towards the building and got my mind focused on today's case.

"We have one more trial, Maya, we're almost there. Can you imagine the kind of attention the firm is going to get after we win this?"

Without waiting for my answer, my partner kept right on talking

"Yeah this is our year," she continued.

Pushing open the door to Sampson Courthouse, a whistle blew in the distance as a police officer signaled everyone to hurry and leave the building. Before it registered to me that a criminal was on the loose, gunshots erupted, and my body began to convulse before I dropped to the ground, shaking. What was happening? As I lay sprawled out on the floor, I looked up and met a familiar pair of eyes as they looked down on me. *Beep Beep Beep*

For a second, I thought I was having an out of body experience, until my eyes opened and I glanced down at my alarm clock. With an attitude, I slapped my clock until it shut off. It was 5:00 a.m. on Monday. With a sigh, I sat upright in my bed. How did things get this bad? For years, I had had the same dream. The man in my nightmares was my biological father, or whom I liked to call, my sperm donor. As a young child, I watched my biological mother get physically and mentally abused by that man. It wasn't until she gave birth to my brother that she realized she needed to get away from that volatile situation. With nowhere to go and no family to call on, we spent months in shelters before finally making the move to Washington, D.C. Somehow he was still able to track our whereabouts and ended up killing the two most important people in my life. I still wondered why he killed them and not me. It was as if he wanted me to stay alive just to suffer. I shuddered at the memories before picking up my cell phone from the nightstand. I needed to call my adopted mother to tell her about the reoccurring nightmare.

Even though it was early, I knew she would answer my call. My adopted parents, whom I simply considered to be my parents, always believed in the saying the early bird catches the worm. On the second ring, my assumption came true as Mom's preppy voice carried through the line. "Good morning, dear."

After my parents and brother were killed, I was blessed enough to be adopted into a very wealthy and loving family. Stephen and Victoria Kincaid were unable to have children. When their housekeeper, Ms. Francis, introduced them to me, they knew immediately that I would be theirs. The Kincaid's were known everywhere as one of the leading black families in America. With feature stories about them in publications such as Black Enterprise and appearing on programs like The Oprah Winfrey Show, members of my family have been asked to do it all.

My father's parents, Brent and Barbara Kincaid, received doctorate degrees from Howard University. After graduating, they started a multi-billion dollar technology company. Once their four children, including my father, were grown, they went on to retire and currently resided in Palm Beach, Florida. As the only one of his siblings not interested in going into the family business, my father, Stephen Kincaid, attended Harvard Law School. After years of hard work, he was appointed as a federal judge in Maryland.

My mother, Victoria, obtained her business degree from Yale, but did not use it a day in her life. Having grown up in New York, mom came from old money that was acquired centuries ago. Instead of working, she joined every charity board on the East Coast, and unfortunately for me, decided to invest her time and energy into my every move.

"Morning Mother," I said with a sigh.

"What's wrong with you sweetie?" her voice immediately turned into concern.

"I had another one of those dreams."

Silence hung in the air as Mother took in this information.

"Well you mustn't let it get you down. You have a high profile case, which will be aired across the nation in a few hours. So snap out of it. What will you be wearing today?"

Squeezing my eyes shut, I wondered why the hell I even bothered sharing my problems with this woman. Taking a deep breath to control my emotions, I responded.

"A navy blue Chanel skirt suit I purchased last week," I said through gritted teeth.

"Chanel? Honey you just wore a Chanel suit when you were a guest legal correspondent on CNN last week. Can we do something different this time? I think that little Givenchy number I bought for you would be perfect, and…"

"Where's dad?" I interrupted. Sitting up in my bed, I imagined her rolling her eyes and handing the phone off to my father. I was a daddy's girl, and it was evident my mother didn't like that.

"How's my superstar doing today?" barked Judge Kincaid in my ear.

Though both my parents were uptight and hard on me, I always appreciated the law connection I shared with my father. After words of encouragement and some advice, I got off the phone, feeling better than I had when I first placed the call. Before I could talk myself into fifteen more minutes of extra sleep, I stood up and slid into my comfy house shoes, hoping a steamy shower and a hot cup of coffee would completely wake me up. Now, its show time.

CHAPTER 5

Court Day (Maya)

Running my hands over my Givenchy suit jacket to straighten any random wrinkles, I quickly let out a deep breath, reapplied my coral pink lipstick, and exited the bathroom. With my soft jet black curls bouncing against the back of my neck and my navy blue Tom Ford pumps clicking across the marble floors of the courthouse, I was confident that the verdict would go in my client's favor. Rushing back to my seat at the defense table, I gave a small reassuring smile to the woman whose life was on the line. Tashana Moore was noticiably nervous, and with good reason. Officers watched her from every corner of the room and were ready to pounce the very second she showed any violent signs. Little did they know, my client wouldn't hurt a fly.

As a mother of two who struggled to raise her two-year-old-and-five-year-old sons alone,

Tashana made the decision to leave them both in a car while she went on a job interview after her babysitter cancelled at the last minute. Once a concerned passerby heard one of the children crying in the beat-up Corolla amidst 90-degree weather, the bystander immediately called the police, and the 22-year-old mother was arrested and thrown in jail. It was then that her sons were released into the system. This was one of the reasons why I decided to become a defense attorney. Although my client should not have left her kids in the car, what else was a desperate mother supposed to do? Did this act automatically label her a bad mother? No, she wasn't. In fact, she was a damn good mother in my book, and that was what I tried to make the jury see.

"Has the jury reached a verdict?"

"Yes, your honor, we have."

Standing slowly, yet with confidence, I motioned for my client to stand as well.

"We, the jury, find the defendant, Tashana Moore, not guilty of child neglect, criminal mistreatment, and reckless endangering."

Before I could react, Tashana threw her arms around my shoulders and cried. Behind us, cheers went around as neighborhood friends and concerned citizens celebrated in our victory. The voices of her sons rang from the back of the courtroom as their grandmother tried to quiet them. "Mommy, come home with us," one of them yelled.

Banging his gavel, Judge Morrison, silenced the court as he gave final words. At the judge's dismissal, Tashana let go of me and made a beeline for her children. Packing up my belongings, it took everything in me not to break down in tears. This woman deserved a chance, and I'm glad the jury believed that too. Once I shook hands and spoke with her family, together we walked towards the front of the courthouse. After being greeted by a crowd of reporters, I happily answered their questions.

"What does this case mean to you, Attorney Kincaid?" a reporter asked.

"This case was bigger than Ms. Moore and me," I responded, looking directly into their camera. "It was for her children, and for single parents everywhere, not just mothers, who do what it takes every single day to make sure they can provide for their children. Thank you, and God bless."

Though crowds continued to circle around Tashana and me, I instructed her to go home. Once I'd made sure she and her family had safely made it to their car, I hopped into mine and told the chauffeur to head straight for the office. Before my driver could pull off, my cell phone rang. Noticing the incoming caller, I happily answered. "Helloooo Judge Kincaid," I sang.

"Now that's my girl!" he yelled through the phone.

Beaming from ear to ear, I heard my mother

yell in the background, "Honey, tell her she did amazing, and that her suit looked absolutely pristine on television." Thanking my parents, I basked in their praise, then hung up to sink into the leather interior of the car. I was excited, but tired as all hell. Those seventy-hour weeks had paid off, now I was ready for a much-needed vacation.

CHAPTER 6

Victory Is Mine (Maya)

"Ms. Kincaid, we're here," said my driver. Jumping up in my seat, I opened the door and rushed into the building of Crawford & Stephenson. Walking into my office, which was on the corner of 18th and Pennsylvania, fellow attorneys congratulated me on my big win. Even Robert Crawford, one of the partners, came out of his plush office to celebrate with me.

"You did great," Rob said as he leaned against my door with his arms folded across his chest. Not one to normally smile, I noticed a hint of a grin come to the curve of his mouth. "Your potential is amazing. I guess growing up with a judge as a father did you some good. I hope you take a little vacation time after this, it's well deserved, Maya."

Grateful that he brought up the vacation time instead of me, I agreed that maybe a week or two would be wonderful to have off. As soon as he left my office, I fell back in my chair and looked at the pictures on my desk. I was surrounded by love but there were still times that I longed for a love unlike any other. My gaze fell on an old worn photo of my late mother. "Hope I'm making you proud Mama," I whispered. When I was first adopted, I noticed immediately the differences between my biological mother and my adopted one. Victoria Kincaid almost had a heart attack when I called her 'Mama' one day. As soon as that word came out of my mouth she led me into the bathroom and made me wash my mouth out with soap. "Speak the King's English," she would tell me. That same day she made it her mission to refine me. Between music lessons, etiquette courses, and debutante balls, Victoria, or mother as I was instructed to call her, was determined to raise me in what she called, the proper way.

The loud chime from my office phone brought me back to the present. "Come out tonight, bitch, it's time to celebrate!" Ivey yelled on the other end.

CHAPTER 7

It's a Celebration Every Time We Link Up (Maya)

"Cheers to success!" Ivey yelled across the table.

Clinking our champagne flutes, we smiled at each other while preparing to enjoy a great meal at a trendy Asian restaurant in Northwest. There was so much to be excited about this evening. Besides my win, Taylor's nonprofit organization *Every Girl Counts,* which focused on providing prom dresses to young girls who couldn't otherwise afford one, had officially launched. I was happy that Taylor was able to pair her fashion expertise with a great cause. Plus, Ivey had a surprise announcement to make. It seemed like things were going great for all three of us. With a wide grin, the shapely waitress, who appeared to be in her mid-30's, asked if we needed anything else. Once she was sure that her table of three giggly women was all set, she moved along to assist other guests.

"Okay ladies," Ivey said with a wide smile. "Remember my trip to L.A. last month? The one where I said I went to visit my cousin?"

Silently, we both nodded, and waited anxiously for her to continue. With a dramatic pause, she slowly sipped from her flute, then cleared her throat. Taye and I rolled our eyes as we sat on the edges of our seats.

"Well, really it was because I went to audition for a co-hosting gig with a new entertainment show on Entertainment Daily. Anyway, I got it!"

Tears came to her eyes as we all yelled in excitement throughout the restaurant. People began to look, but we didn't care. For years, Ivey dreamed of becoming a big entertainment talk show host, and it was finally happening! To be seen on a show airing on a leading network was enough to ensure the start of a major television career. Running back to the table to make sure everything was okay, our waitress politely asked us to keep it down; but none of us really cared to. Ivey was about to become the star that we all knew she would be. While Taylor shot our almost-famous friend a million questions, my mind drifted down memory lane. In fact, there was one particular memory of Ivey and me when we were sixteen that came to mind.

"Yeah, I always knew I was special," an overly confident Ivey once beamed to a small group of

11th grade admirers at the lunch table. I rolled my eyes as I braced myself to hear yet another self-proclaimed superstar story from my best friend. With her round hazel eyes, chocolate complexion, and coke-bottle shaped body, Ivey Walden was without a doubt the dream of every teenage boy in the DMV.

"I'm destined for greatness."

And despite her rough upbringing, she was. Growing up in Southeast, Ivey saw firsthand the power of drugs. With a mother who was a stripper and prostitute and a father who was too strung out on the pipe to be around, Ivey was what some people would call a diamond in the rough. Raised by her grandmother, who was also likely to smoke an occasional joint, Ivey found solitude in writing and theatre. Every time she would present poetry or a short story, she demonstrated beauty, grace, excitement, and pure talent.

She was also one of the smartest kids in the area, and was awarded a full academic and hardship scholarship to the exclusive Bradwel Preparatory School, which was where we eventually met. Back then, my group of friends hated her. They called her a charity case and said she was too poor to hang out with us. I was her only true girlfriend at school and we became as thick as thieves, against my mother's approval, of course. Mother always preferred that I stayed close with the President's daughter or some other child from an affluent family, similar to ours. As the three of us chatted more about our hopes and dreams while sitting at the table, an unknown number with a New York area code flashed across my screen.

"Hello?" I asked.

"Hi, is this Maya?" the voice questioned on the other end.

"Yes, may I ask who's calling?"

"It's Vince. Vincent James, I met you a few weeks ago at Club 14th Street."

Out of shock, I almost spit my drink out. Had this gorgeous man really taken the time to look for me? Quickly excusing myself from the table, I walked towards the ladies room while trying to figure out why he was so interested. I knew I was a cute woman, but I seemed kind of average next to those girls I saw hanging on ball players' arms.

"Hey, what's up? I'm out at dinner right now."

"Well, I don't want to hold you up. I was just hoping that I could take you to dinner sometime this weekend."

Placing my bag against the sink in the bathroom, I grabbed my brush to straighten up, as if Vince could somehow see me. A silence hung in the air until he nervously continued.

"If you're interested, just let me know what day and time works for you."

Maybe it was the vision of his beautiful smile and athletic frame that made my mouth speak before my mind processed what was going on.

"I'll be ready at 8:00 p.m. this Saturday. Is this your cell number? I'll text my address to this number."

"Great," he said excitedly. "See you then."

I ended my call and walked back to the table. Ivey and Taye looked on patiently as they waited to hear the details of the secret caller.

"That was Vince from the club last weekend," I said dismissively. "We're going on a date this Saturday."

"Yes!" yelled Ivey with a fist pump. "My girl hasn't been out with a good man in forever. It's about time you decided to move on. Plus, Vince is an excellent candidate. I'm happy I gave him your number."

Ivey paused briefly, making me realize she was referring to moving on from my first love. A part of me wanted a relationship with someone while another part still just wasn't ready.

"Why didn't you ask me first?" I asked her, purposely ignoring her reference.

"Because I know you. Plus he's Damien Roseland's fine ass agent, and he bribed me for your number in exchange for an interview. So, yeah I threw you under the bus. You're welcome."

A slight sigh of relief escaped me when I learned Vince wasn't a basketball player. His occupation made the chances of him cheating a little bit less. Shocked at what my girl would do for an interview, I was thankful that I was able to finally have a date with a man outside of Urbanmatch.com. I had dated two dudes previously from the site and they all ended in shambles.

"Remember the dude you met a few weeks ago on that website?" Taye began, reading my mind.

Of course I remembered him:

Why did I continue to subject myself to online dating, I thought to myself as I waited for my mystery guest to appear. Glancing down nervously at my freshly painted nails, I couldn't help but notice that my date was already ten minutes late.

"Hmm, not even a phone call," I huffed. Another five minutes went by until the brother appeared in a tight suit and colorful tie. Yes, his pecan brown complexion and chiseled face was handsome, but his taste in clothes made him look cheap and like a throwback pimp. To top things off, his profile listed him as 6"1, but I could tell his ass was barely pushing 5"7. Pissed but determined to make something out of our night, I plastered a friendly smile on my face and stood to greet my date, Terrance. Ignoring my outstretched hand, Terrance grabbed me into a tight hug, while damn near crushing my ribs, and said, "Damn baby, you fine!"

Though some women would have been flattered, I was not. Jumping out of his arms, I shot him a look and sat back down in my seat. In an effort to remain light hearted and fun, qualities my previous dates said I lacked, I let Terrance know that since he was running a little behind, I took the liberty of ordering our appetizer.

"Cool," he smiled, displaying a perfect set of white teeth. Relaxing a bit, I continued. "Yeah, the stuffed mushrooms here are pretty good, I'm sure you'll like them.

"Ah, hell no. Them things give a nigga gas. Unless you want me blowing up this restaurant you need to order something different. They ain't got chicken wings in here?"

"This is an Italian restaurant, no they don't have wings in here."

"You one of them stuck-up chicks, hunh? We coulda just went to Ruby Tuesdays or IHop, but your fancy ass dragged me all the way out to Georgetown when all a nigga wants is chicken."

Before I could respond, our waitress appeared. I'm sure it was because Terrance was so loud that nearby patrons were starting to look our way.

"What can I get for you both?" the waitress asked.

Squinting at her name tag, my unruly date looked up at the waitress and simply said," Christina, cancel that nasty ass order of mushrooms, and get us wings for an appetizer. Then my girl over here can stand to lose a pound or two so get her a Caesar salad, then get me the steak and shrimp platter."

Caught off guard, Christina cleared her throat and told the cheap bastard, like I already had, that they didn't have fried chicken. Still shocked that this low budget man had basically called me fat, I sat motionless until I snapped out of my trance and told Mr. Cheap-o that I had to use the bathroom. Instead, I raced out of the restaurant like a bat out of hell. There was no way I was going to sit with that man for any longer. Plus, I knew at this rate, he would probably stick me with the bill at the end anyway.

Reliving the date with my girls, I began digging into my pasta. The only thing going through my mind was, "Later for Terrance, what am I going to wear with Vince?"

CHAPTER 8

California Love (Maya)

The next day, the three of us crowded inside of Ivey's two-bedroom apartment. In a panic, Ivey had called us both early in the morning, begging for help with her packing. She was expected to be in L.A. by noon the next day and was told by her agent that the movers would arrive to get her things by 3:00 p.m. that day. Opening the door, I could tell that her nerves had gotten the best of her. Her eyes were red, her hair was all over her head, and she was sweating through her V-neck t-shirt. The sight of the poor girl made me laugh. Soon, I had Taye giggling too. In the entrance of her apartment, we both held each other up as we cracked up looking at the scene before us. Annoyed, Ivey threw some boxes our way and became dramatic, as always. At this rate, she was going to make a killing in Hollywood.

"Nothing is funny," she seethed through clenched teeth. "What are ya'll laughing about?"

Finally catching my breath, I took a MAC compact out of my purse and held up the mirror for Ivey to look into.

"We're laughing at you!"

Doubling over again, Taylor and I cried dime-sized tears.

"How are you having a breakdown and haven't even been to Hollywood yet?" I asked.

Leaving us to laugh our little hearts away, Ivey stormed into her bedroom where she blasted her music and continued to pack.

"Let's go help the drama queen," Taye said. "Oh Lord, I can just imagine how this girl will act once she has had a couple of shows and more interviews under her belt."

With smirks, we both went to help Hurricane Ivey. Walking in the room before me, Taylor gasped and ran to Ivey's side. Lying on the floor with her head hanging low and tears seeping through her fingers, Ivey's shoulders shook in despair. Turning to silence her stereo, we were confused about what was going on. Walking toward her, I crouched on her other side and smoothed down her hair in an attempt to calm her down. No one said anything; instead, we sat there, waiting for our friend to gather her thoughts. Slowly she lifted her head and began to roughly wipe her face. It was almost as if she were upset about letting her feelings out.

"What's going on?" I asked.

Finally dropping her hands after wiping away

the tears, she spoke to us.

"I've lived out here my whole life. Yeah, I've visited other places, but this is my home. What if I leave and mess up? What if I'm not ready for this? I've been through so much already, and I just can't blow this opportunity. Do I even deserve this? I'm afraid. Plus, I won't have you guys there."

Turning so that she had Ivey's hands in her own, Taylor answered.

"You are beautiful, ambitious, and have a heart of gold. You deserve this chance more than anyone I know. You can't break down now; it's only the beginning. You inspire me every day. We're a lot alike, but what I admire most about you is how positive you stay. Sometimes I get stuck in the hurt from my past, but you have never done that and now you finally have an entertainment platform where you can connect with even more people, and younger ones who may have experienced the kind of things you have. Ivey, this is your calling."

A few hours later, Ivey was packed up and ready to go.

CHAPTER 9

The Police Report (Janet)

"I-I-I came to file a police report," said the nervous actress to the officer. "Whom may I speak with?"

In the tiny room at the local police department, her sudden announcement was met with complete silence, dropped mouths, and intense stares. For what seemed like hours, Janet stood planted in her spot, looking ready to run out of the room at any minute. Finally, unable to keep his mouth shut, an officer jumped up from his seat in the corner of the small office.

"Aren't you that actress?"

Without looking up, Janet visibly trembled. In her head, she could still feel the pain that she had endured just a few days earlier. Finally, she looked up, displaying a black eye that barely opened and red scratches on her neck. Just looking at the bruise to the right side of her face one would know that she needed medical attention. As she glanced around the room, a female officer finally stood up and motioned for Janet to follow her. Looking like she had the weight of the world on her shoulders, Janet allowed the officer to lead the way to a quiet room. As the pair met, eyes peeked through the blinds from the room she had just walked out of. Something was terribly wrong. The door was slightly ajar and those in the room were able to hear her tearful cries.

"I was raped!"

CHAPTER 10

Wine and Dine (Maya)

My doorbell rang promptly at 8:00 p.m. Rushing to spray on my favorite fragrance, I grabbed my clutch and took one more glance into my full-length mirror. Not bad, I thought to myself as I fluffed out my spiral curls. Wearing hip-hugging black leather pants, a long black sheer blouse, and my newest pair of electric blue Jimmy Choo's, I knew my date wouldn't be disappointed. Rushing to the door, I felt nervous. This would be my first real date, outside of online dating, with someone in more than three years.

"Hey Maya," Vince said as I opened the door. In his hands rested a pink gift bag.

"Come in," I said, my eyes taking in the fine man in front of me. He made slacks and a simple black dress shirt look incredibly sexy. Finally, my eyes rested on the bag again. Noticing my stare, Vince handed me the present and sat on one of the bar chairs in the kitchen.

"I think flowers are cliché, so I wanted to give

you something different. Open it up."

Anxiously, I sat the gift down on my marble kitchen countertop and started to tear through the tissue paper. Inside was something much more meaningful to me than flowers.

"*Fight Back and Win: My 30-Year Fight Against Injustice and How You Can Win Your Own Battles*, by Gloria Allred," I read aloud with a huge grin. "How did you know I'm obsessed with her?"

"It's only all on your Facebook profile," he said with a grin. "You know I did my homework on you before I asked you out."

With excitement, a smile stretched across my face.

"That was very sweet of you, she's my favorite attorney, besides my father of course. Thank you."

Grabbing my keys and last minute items, Vince sat on my couch and marveled at my condo. "This place is nice," he whistled softly.

Smiling at him, I was used to people complimenting my condominium. It was a two million dollar property with two bedrooms, a loft, and a spiral staircase that added a vintage feel to my otherwise modern place. At the insistence of my mother, I had hired the famous interior decorator, Samantha Francois, and she had done an amazing job. With beige and gold accents, my home was classy, yet fun. Everyone who came to visit immediately fell in love.

"Thanks, you ready to go?"

"Of course, we have reservations."

"Where to?" Since setting up our date, Vince had refused to tell me where he was taking me.

"It's a surprise, just relax."

I wasn't big on surprises, but decided to just go with the flow. Touching my elbow, he led us out the door and to his car. Once settled inside the high-priced sports car, Vince looked over and admired me.

"You look beautiful tonight, by the way."

"Thank you," I said. "And you look very handsome."

"I'm surprised you're being so nice. I expected you to be mean. I thought you would be like you were when I first met you. You weren't rude, but just really short with me."

"I'm sorry," I said with a thoughtful pause. "That's not normally me."

"Good to know," Vince smiled.

During the twenty-minute car ride, the two of us sang along to the slow jams on the radio, made small talk and laughed. It had been a while since I could be myself around someone other than family and friends, and it felt good. Before we knew it, we were in front of a Sushi and Hibachi restaurant.

"Wow this place looks packed," I said with an approving nod.

"It's always packed."

Though the restaurant was crowded, we were

seated in no time in what seemed to be a secluded area. Moments later, our orders were taken and a band came into the room to serenade us with some smooth jazz.

"So, what made you become a sports agent?" I asked, trying to make conversation. I couldn't quite make out Vince's look as he slowly glanced up at me from his menu.

"I was drafted right out of my second year of college. After a few years, I had something like a freak accident and messed up my knee. Long story short, after that happened I decided to stay in the industry and represent athletes."

"Oh, okay. I'm sorry to hear about your injury, but glad you're still able to be in the business that you love."

"Well, I'm just glad to be here," he said as he reached across the table for my hand.

Blushing, I felt a vibration on the table. Vince quickly picked his phone up off of the table, turned it on silent and apologized.

"I'm sorry, my full attention is on you tonight."

"So we ignore calls now, Vincent?" a sharp and snooty voice said from behind me.

As I looked up to see to whom this voice belonged to, I noticed a pretty girl with a Halle Berry knockoff haircut standing next to our table.

"Hey Shannon, how are you?" Vince asked nervously. "Oh, um Shannon this is Maya. Maya, Shannon."

"Nice to meet you," I said as I stretched out

my hand to shake hers.

With a look of disgust gracing her otherwise beautiful face, our intruder ignored my outstretched hand and continued to speak with Vince as if I were invisible.

"So, why haven't you called me back? I've been trying to reach you for two weeks. You know I just bought a place out here."

"Shannon, this is a bad time. Can I give you a call sometime this week? We can talk then."

Both amused and irritated at the conversation happening in front of me, I began to realize that this girl was definitely one of Vince's old flings. She obviously didn't know who I was.

"Sharon, I'll make sure Vince calls you this week," I said to her with a syrupy smile.

"It's Shannon. Shannon Drayson," she snapped. "And don't worry about it, I no longer want the call. He had his chance."

"Well honey, obviously you do if you've been trying to reach him for two weeks."

A quiet Vince sat back and watched us go back and forth as if he were watching a tennis match.

"Girl please," Shannon began. "You seem like a smart lady. It would probably be in your best interest to get away from this man and anyone else associated with him while you still have a chance. If not, please believe I'll see you again."

With that, she smirked and walked off to sit at a table in an adjoining room with two men in dark suits. The crew shot us dark looks the rest of the night. When she was away from the table, I faced Vince and gave him the look of death. Not only was the woman rude, but she had pretty much just threatened me.

"So that's your type? Bitchy and Rude?"

Yes, she was gorgeous as all hell, and I definitely recognized her newest edition Blue Indigo Matte Hermes Birkin bag that she wore on her shoulder, but she got me messed up. In my mind I made a mental note to ask my father to buy me the same purse, but in black.

"I'm so sorry. I went out with her a couple of times, but I didn't feel it going anywhere so I kind of just started ignoring her."

I could sense his nervousness as he spoke. Shaking my head, I downed my Merlot and concentrated on my dish. In between a mouthful of sushi I looked up and simply said, "Don't make me regret giving you a try."

After several seconds of silence, I noticed Vince's eyes blazing a hole through me.

"You really are beautiful," he said, as if sensing my uncertainty.

Relaxing a little, I basked in his compliment. "Thanks. Is that why you finally found my number and called?"

"Actually, I got your number that same night I met you. Ivey gave it to me."

"So why'd it take you so long to call?" I asked as I shook my head and smiled at Ivey's involvement in setting me up.

"Well, after you left the club, your friends were telling me and my friend about how busy you were with work. I figured you'd have more time to hang out after your big case was over. Congrats on that by the way. I saw you on T.V."

"Thank you! This case was really crazy but all the hard work paid off," I beamed with pride.

"That's what's up! Beauty and brains, just what I like."

CHAPTER 11

Infatuation (Vince)

I was excited about the woman sitting beside me. She was everything I looked for in a woman – stunning, smart, driven, and self-sufficient. Most of the females, who paid attention to me were the ones who knew and only cared about my occupation and connections. I couldn't stop staring at Maya's smooth and blemish free, brown complexion, almond shaped eyes, and draping hair. I'm no hair expert, but I would bet that her hair was the real deal instead of being all weaved-up. When I walked behind her, my eyes landed on her ass every time. It's like the girl woke up and went to sleep doing squats, but I wasn't complaining. I appreciate women who take care of their bodies.

"Thanks for dinner, the food was delicious. I have to go back again one day," Maya said, after we left the restaurant and were in my car.

"Glad you liked it."

Taking my right hand off the steering wheel,

I decided to boldly rest it on her lap. Pulling up in front of her house, I noticed she was getting fidgety.

"Do you want to go for a walk?" she asked nervously. "There's a lake and park right down the street."

It was getting late into the night, but the lights surrounding us from the different lampposts illuminated her neighborhood. I could see the park sign pointing ahead.

"I wish I could, but I have meetings early in the morning."

I watched as her face fell, but she quickly tried to recover with a smile.

"Okay, well thanks again, I really had a nice time with you."

"Of course, I hope you let me take you out again sometime soon."

I hopped out the car to open her door. After a brief hug, I walked her to the front door and patiently waited as she anxiously scanned her badge against the key coder. Once she was safely in her home and the door was shut, I stood silently for a second. The whole ride home, Maya was all I could think about. It was something about this girl. Grabbing my phone, I dialed her number. I was close to home, but just had to hear her voice one last time.

"Will you let me come back tomorrow evening so we can take that walk?" I asked when she picked up.

"Yes, I'd like that." I could hear her smile through the phone, and that alone made me smile too.

CHAPTER 12

Back to Reality (Maya)

Leaning against my door, I couldn't believe how well my date had gone. Of course, there was the minor glitch with the girl interrupting our meal, but other than that, Vince had been the perfect gentleman. *Okay Maya, don't rush things here*, I silently said to myself. Here I was, at the height of my career and I didn't have time to sit around entertaining some guy.

"Maybe I need to cut this charade short now. I have too many things going on and a man would just complicate things."

Before I could finish my thoughts, my phone rang, with Vince's number flashing across my screen. Without realizing it, a smile crept to my face and I slowly answered it.

"Hey you," I said flirtatiously, out of nowhere. Before I knew it, Vince had invited himself over the next night to visit the park. Of course, I accepted, the man was fine! As soon as I hung up, I did a twirl into the kitchen, almost knocking over the white trash can. Two minutes later, my phone rang again with my colleague, Attorney Charles Donaldson, on the other end. Still high off life, I answered the call with a huge grin.

"Hey Chuck!" I enthusiastically greeted him.

"Hi Maya. I'm sorry to bother you so late, but I wanted to see if you could help me with a domestic violence case. I really need your help. I know it's the weekend, but I wanted to see if we could meet up tomorrow?"

Instantly, my joy deflated as reality hit me once again. I was given time off from work, but I knew I would only get better with practice.

"Of course I can," I responded. After agreeing to meet Chuck the next day, I hung up, and quickly sent Vince a text.

I have to work late tomorrow; maybe we can go out again some other time.

Remembering my priorities, I pushed Send and ran to my room to figure out what I was going to wear to the office the following day. It was an off day and I knew many people wouldn't be in tomorrow, but I still wanted to look my best. There was work to be done, and no man could distract me from it. Besides, the last man who tried to, left me.

CHAPTER 13

Bad News (Vince)

"Dang," I mumbled after reading Maya's text for the third time. I was looking forward to spending time with her, but she'd sent a message saying she would be at work the following day. I was used to girls dropping all their plans for me. Doctor's appointments, work, phone calls, whatever. Before I could think further, my phone rang, with my number one client's name etched across the screen.

"Man, I need you to turn to a news channel now!"Damien yelled on the other end. Confused at where this was going, I grabbed my remote and flipped to the network. Before I could tune-in, he hung up.

I felt like a ton of bricks had fallen on me as I stared at the Fox Breaking News report that ran across my big screen.

ACTRESS AND MODEL, JANET
SPRINGER REPORTEDLYRAPED.
TROUBLED NBA PLAYER, DAMIEN
ROSELAND, CONSIDERED THE MAIN
SUSPECT.

Almost as soon as I finished reading the headline, I heard my phone go off. I was certain that those were calls from the press looking for an interview. Ignoring all of them, I stood and rushed to call Damien back. This was a huge problem. After two rings, followed by no answer, I decided it would be best to just head on over to his house. An hour later, I pulled up outside his new bachelor pad in Ashburn, Virginia, a suburban area just outside of the city. Silencing my engine, I heard music blasting from inside the house and saw women of different ethnicities lounging inside the gates of Damien's pool area. For several minutes, I sat in the car, wondering if it were best for me to go inside. Finally, I reasoned that it was in the best interest of my client to go indoors and speak with him. Even before I climbed out of the car and hit the front porch, an Asian beauty, barely clad in a string bikini, stopped me in my tracks with a fruit tray in her hands.

"Would you like a chocolate covered strawberry, sir?"

Though her lips looked soft enough to kiss, and her body was banging, I pushed past her and went straight to the front door. There was business to be handled.

Huffing away from me, the hostess took her curves and strawberries and stormed back inside the gate to the pool party. As expected, my knocks became lost in the sounds of hip-hop music. Instead of waiting for someone to let me in, I pushed the large oak door open until I was greeted by the empty foyer.

"Damien," I yelled. "It's Vince, where you at?"

"Upstairs man," he responded after a few seconds.

Taking two stairs at a time, I expected Damien to be flanked by groupies. Instead, he sat alone on his balcony, overlooking his pool party with a lit cigar in his mouth. Even after clearing my throat to announce my presence, Damien never looked away from the scene happening outside. Without saying a word, he passed me the cigar. We sat side-by-side, him lost in his thoughts, and I giving him time to gather them.

"I didn't do it," he said after several moments went by. "I actually loved her, man."

Without knowing all the facts of the situation, I knew Damien wasn't responsible. "I know you didn't rape her. Which is why we need to act fast and clear your name."

Finally looking at me, I noticed my twenty-three-year-old basketball sensation had been crying. Expecting him to reveal a deep dark secret or some insight as to why he was a suspect, I was shocked by my client's next words, "Thank you, it's rare that anyone ever believes in me outside of basketball."

It was my business to make sure the athletes I signed were taken care of. In spite of this being the biggest obstacle of my ten-year professional career as an agent, this situation would be no different. An hour later, the police entered his house and Damien was arrested. Promising to post bail for him and to stop the party that was going on at his property, I watched as my young star was escorted to jail. Sitting on his couch, I considered the next steps that needed to be taken. After a quick phone call, I couldn't help but grin. Things were going as planned. Before I left his house, I found the original Asian chick and took the strawberry she had offered me, plus a little more. Hours later, I figured it was time for me to post bail and get Damien out.

CHAPTER 14

Work Relations (Maya)

"Alright Chuck I think you're good to go with this."

It was late at night and I was tired to the bone. The case I was asked to help with seemed elementary, but Charles Donaldson, the attorney assigned to it, kept asking questions, as if he hadn't been practicing law for years. *I could have had my day off for all this*, I thought to myself.

"Well thank you for all your help," Chuck smiled as I gathered my computer and briefcase. "Please let me take you to dinner to show my appreciation."

"Oh, no," I responded with a twinkle in my eye. "An Espresso from Starbucks will work just fine."

His laugh rang through the office, before his face turned serious. "No, Maya, what if I wanted to take you on a kind-of-romantic dinner?" Walking towards me, he attempted to pull me into his embrace, but my strong arms, compliments of Jeannete Jenkins' new workout DVD, pushed him away. Warning bells went off inside my head.

This is why he wanted my assistance, I concluded. This explained why he reached out for my help, and then was asking simple questions that he probably already knew the answers to. Glaring at the lanky and middle-aged white man standing next to me with his wedding ring dangling from his left hand, I concentrated on not cussing him out for being disrespectful and wasting my time. Once I gathered my thoughts, I walked to the door and said, "I don't date co-workers, plus I'm sure your wife wouldn't appreciate that. Have a good night, counselor."

Rushing to my car in the parking garage, I felt heat rush to my face. Before even starting the car, I hit the call button next to Taylor's name. When my call went to voicemail, I threw the car in reverse and exited the garage. I was pissed; this wasn't the first time one of my co-workers had hit on me, and frankly, it was getting old. Luckily, I lived close to my office, and was home in four minutes. Once I entered my bedroom, I snatched the clothes off my body and raced into my bathroom to run a much-needed bubble bath. As soon as I slid into the bubbles, with candles lit and champagne poured into a nearby glass, my phone rang. Eyes closed, I shouted out, "Answer" to signal my wireless prompter in the bathroom to pick up the call.

"Hey, girl!" Ivey yelled.

"Yeah, what's up?"

"Damn, somebody's got their panties in a bunch today."

Ignoring her sarcasm, I sank deeper into my Jacuzzi tub as hot gusts of water hit my tense body in every direction.

"Anyway, guess who gets to interview Viola Davis and Morris Chestnut?" she squealed. "Cali is great, I'm never coming back! I even met a man out here, girl. But anyway, the reason why I called was to thank you for going out with that guy, Vince. Seems like shit has really hit the fan with Damien Roseland, and they want me to interview him for an article in *Sports* Magazine, can you believe it? A well-known actress was raped and he's a suspect, so now they're trying to clear his name. Obviously it's not good for him, but that article will be great for my career!"

At the mention of Vince, my attention was immediately grabbed and I began to feel bad for the situation that he and his client were in.

"Wow," I started. "Based on what the media is reporting, does it look like Damien is guilty?"

"Oh, definitely, the evidence is strong. But of course as a journalist, I need to go in there unbiased. Vince asked me to paint a picture of a good guy who comes from bad circumstances, but no one tells me how to write. I go based on the facts, so I'll gauge him during our interview next week. If everything goes well, this could be listed as one of my top interviews. Of course the interview with the First Lady still ranks as my best," my friend beamed through the phone.

For another ten minutes, we updated each other on our various projects. She had gotten settled in L.A. and was working nonstop with her co-host and the network. Eventually, I figured it was time to get off the phone and to jump out the tub before I turned into a prune. After hanging up from our call, I texted my mother to let her know I would be at our home in the Hamptons the next morning. Knowing she would be pleased, I made reservations to use the personal family jet and dozed off.

CHAPTER 15

Home Sweet Home (Maya)

"We are now descending into Southampton."

Waking up, I did a quick stretch and looked at the scenery below. It was beautiful. After representing clients from all backgrounds, including doing pro bono work for those who couldn't afford my services, such as Tashana, I began to truly appreciate my life. I was a trust fund baby, but wanted to be so much more. I became a lawyer, not because of the money, because I had plenty of it already, but because I wanted to make a difference in the lives of others. Similar to the difference Ms. Francis made in mine when my family died all those years ago. I typically represented people who were looked at as underdogs, because at one time I was considered to be one.

"Honey, I'm so glad you made it," my mother shrieked in her Adidas sweat suit as I exited the plane. In one arm she held Brockman, her three-year-old Shih Tzu, and with the other she grabbed me into a tight hug. I could tell she was trying to smile but couldn't, thanks to her latest Botox treatment.

"Welcome home, dear," she continued with an exaggerated sweep of her arm. Martin, our long time security guard ran up next to me to grab my bags, but I stopped him and demanded that he give me a hug. Martin had been with our family since way before I was even adopted. In my eyes, he was family.

Ms. Francis, the elderly woman who helped me the night my biological parents and brother died, was once part of our family as well. For fourteen years, she cooked and cleaned for us; however, she was actually much more than just a maid. I would fondly refer to her as my grandmother. Once I was adopted, my parents moved my grandmother into their PG County mansion so that she could remain by my side at all times. That meant a lot to me. If it weren't for her I would have probably been in what people call the "system" or foster care. Plus, she knew my biological family before they were killed, so it was nice to have someone around me who was somewhat familiar with my previous life. Sadly, when I turned seventeen, grandma died from breast cancer. That was without a doubt one of the saddest times of my life. Though she left me with a lot of things, perhaps the most precious gift she gave me was a heart-shaped locket with a photo of us together. Scared to ever lose it, the locket usually remained inside my jewelry box, but whenever I needed strength, I put it on.

"You look well Little Maya," Martin excitedly said. Little Maya was his nickname for me, ever since he heard me recite an old Maya Angelou poem. He always said my name was fitting. He always knew I would either be a poet, performer, or public speaker. When I became a lawyer, he decided my choice of occupation was fitting as well.

"So do you, Martin."

Since the private runway was in the backyard of our sprawling estate, it only took a few steps for us to reach the back door of the house. Pushing through the glass screen, I headed straight for my father's study.

"Daddy!" I yelled. One would think I was ten instead of twenty-nine, judging by the way I ran into my father's arms.

"Hey, darling," the six-foot, two-hundred-seventy-pound intimidating image said to me. To past boyfriends, he was a terror, but to me he was just a big ole' teddy bear. I admit it felt good to be home. Once I looked around and hugged Ms. Mildred, the maid we hired after my grandmother died, I headed up to my room to get settled. With the TV news blasting in the distance, highlighting the Damien Roseland story, my mind went to Vince. I hadn't heard from him since our date.

I was wondering how he was doing with all that was going on with Damien.

"Knock, knock" my mother said as she stood at my door with Brockman still in her arms.

"Honey," she said while walking inside without an invite, "I asked Joseph Stanford to stop by and keep you company this evening. It's about time you move on from the past and get a good man; a real man unlike Josh."

Rolling my eyes upwards to the vaulted ceilings, I took a deep breath to brace my shaking hands. Why did she always have to bring up Josh? I should have known my mother would bring men around the house to hint at me about moving on and getting married. What did she not get? I was not ready. Yes, I went on dates every now and then, but my heart wasn't totally healed from my first love. With a tight smile, I promised her that it wouldn't be necessary since I would be meeting up with my old friend Tinsley after our family dinner.

"Tinsley Tyson?" she questioned. "That girl who was in Jack and Jill with you and is now on that trashy reality show? What is it called again, 'Hip-Hop exes?' I don't think it's a good idea for you to even be associated with someone like that."

"Well, it's a good thing that I'm grown, Mother. I'm meeting her in the city after dinner. Since I have a key to the house you won't need to worry about me getting in after hours."

"Honey, Southampton is a couple of hours away…"

"I'll be staying with Tinsley overnight at her dad's place on the Upper Eastside," I quickly replied while cutting her off. Pursing her lips, Mother did an about-face and left me alone in my room without another word. Good, I thought. *I refuse to let her run me crazy during this visit.* Hours went by while I took a much-needed nap.

"Maya," Ms. Mildred called. "It's time for dinner. You know you've gotta eat while the meal is hot and fresh."

As a child, I remembered my grandmother swatting my legs whenever I came to dinner late. With those memories on my mind, I jumped up, gargled with Listerine, washed my hands, brushed my hair, and headed straight for the dining room table.

"Glad to see you still have the manners your grandmother taught you," Ms. Mildred, or Ms. Milly as we sometimes called her, said with a pleased smile. With the table set and dinner laid out, Father, Mother, Ms. Milly, Martin, and I sat down, ready to eat. Like I said, we were all family. Even Brockman sat quietly in his cage next to the table. It felt good to get an update about everyone's families. Not only did Ms. Milly welcome a new granddaughter a month ago, but Martin's daughter, the youngest of four, was starting her first year in college. All seemed to be going well for everyone.

"Honey, tell Maya that hanging out with Joseph would be better than going out with that Tinsley girl," my mother started.

An uncomfortable silence hung in the air as Mr. Kincaid decided the best way to stay out of the mother-daughter quarrel. "Well, Maya," he began. But before he could continue, a cell phone went off at the table. Apologetically, I stood to take the call, with my father leaning back in his seat, noticeably relieved. Pushing talk, I mouthed an apology and headed into the living room. Who was calling me this late in the evening? My caller ID didn't list a number.

"Maya Kincaid," I started.

On the other end, Vince breathed a sigh of relief.

"Maya, it's Vince here," he started. With no reply, he continued, "Not sure if you've heard the news yet, but my client Damien is being looked at as a suspect for a rape crime that he did not commit. At the arraignment, he pled 'not guilty' and was released. Though we have a great lawyer on payroll, we wanted to discuss the possibility of you taking on this particular case. His trial date is in a few months and we would like to have you by his side."

"Well," I began. "I want to make sure you know that I have not taken on a celebrity case of this caliber before…"

Noting my hesitation Vince interrupted. "Well, the last case you won, made national attention,

I'm sure this wouldn't be any different."

Before I could decline, Vince continued. "What if we met with you tomorrow morning, at your office and then you can make your decision?"

"I'm actually in the Hamptons on vacation."

"What if my client and I meet you out there?"

The question hung in the air while I weighed the pros and cons on taking on the case. "Okay, I'll text you the address of a café where we can meet."

Hanging up, I texted the address of a nearby coffee shop and headed back to the dining room, wondering if this case would help or hurt my career. Regardless, I was dedicated to at least hearing Mr. Roseland out.

CHAPTER 16

When Old Friends Return
(Maya)

"It's about time you came out with me," Tinsley yelled over the loud music.

Since middle school, Tinsley and I had been close. As the heir to Tyson's Jewels, my good friend never really had to worry about money or a career. Her mother, like mine, taught her the art of being an educated stay-at-home mom and trophy wife. Together, we vowed to be much more than a man's arm candy. With me focused on law, and her on medicine, we were two of the smartest kids in school. We were also two of the only black kids. Unfortunately, halfway through the tenth grade Tinsley became a cokehead and would often ditch me to party with her newfound friends and her drug dealer boyfriend. It was then that I grew closer to Ivey, who was a scholarship student at our prestigious private school, and I grew further away from Tinsley, my childhood best friend.

Reading my mind, Tinsley curled up her lip and asked about Ivey. "How's the charity case doing?"

"Don't talk about my girl," I snapped. "While you were busy shaking your ass and snorting coke, screwing me over every time you got the chance, Ivey was the one who stayed by my side and was like a sister to me."

Sitting her glass down on the table in front of us, Tinsley turned to me and apologized.

"I know I haven't been a good friend to you. You were the only person who pushed me to do good things and actually believed in me, and I just had to ruin that. Now all my so-called girlfriends aren't anywhere to be found."

While I had gone on to further my education, Tinsley decided to make it into the reality TV world after finishing high school. She was a beautiful girl with an All-American look, plus she made friends wherever she went. She could also be somewhat of a mean girl though. In college, she did hurtful things, such as gluing Ivey's locker shut, just because she was jealous of our friendship. So far, she'd had four successful shows, but something about her seemed tired and worn down.

"I've missed you, girl," Tinsley continued. Knowing that she needed me, I grabbed her into a tight hug, as if to reassure her that I wasn't going anywhere. Looking at me for several seconds, she finally released a smile that lit up the entire club. As she showcased her million-dollar dimples, a camera flashed in the distance and her smile slowly faded and became a look of irritation.

"Don't they ever get tired?" she complained.

Knowing that she was referring to the paparazzi, I grabbed her elbow and motioned for her to sit down in the booth with me.

"You know you signed up for this lifestyle, right?"

Playing with the cherry in her martini, Tinsley looked into her glass, instead of giving me eye contact, and remained silent.

"I mean, what do you expect? I invited you to my parents' home but you insisted on us coming here. We're in NYC at one of the hottest clubs, one that you chose to come to, and you're irritated that the paparazzi are out here taking pictures of someone who's been all over their television screens for years?"

To me, she sounded silly. She had to know that she would be hounded when we came out tonight.

"I know, I guess I just want a change."

"Well, what do you want now?"

Finally looking up at me, Tinsley had tears in her eyes. "I've been sober for a couple years now, I know you've probably read something different in the tabloids, but I am trying."

Stunned that my best-friend-turned-party girl was opening up to me, the only thing I could do was place my drink down and continue to listen to her.

"The things I've done, I'm not proud of. The only reason why I've gotten away with those things is because of my last name and bank account. Maya, I've been a promiscuous drug addict over the years. I still want to go to med school. I want to save lives but I'm too old now."

"Tins, we're the same age," I told her softly. "You can make that happen."

"Yeah, but I don't know how."

In VIP, we were one of the few people seated, but I noticed a man leaning towards our conversation.

"Do you know him?" I whispered in her ear while subtly pointing at the man standing near us.

"Oh shit, that looks like one of the guys from that gossip blog."

Immediately, tears came back to her eyes, making me protective and angry. "Stay here."

Standing up from the booth, I turned in the direction of our audience and walked swiftly up to him. With his back now turned towards me I tapped him on his shoulder and asked, "What did you hear?"

Realizing that his cover was blown, he let out a deep breath and repeated our whole conversation.

"How much do you need in order not to repeat anything that you heard tonight?"

Barely breathing, our skinny spectator softly said, "Fifty thousand."

"Great! I will draw up a quick confidentiality agreement, with check included, and I expect this conversation to stay out of your little blog. May I remind you of your annual salary? This check will be more money than you will ever see in your lifetime. Remember that, and stay on my good side."

Strutting back to my seat, with Tinsley sitting uneasy and expecting an answer, I wrote out a check, with an agreement on the notepad I keep in my purse and had Mr. Anthony Grossman, sign it. My motto was, "Don't fuck with me or mines, because you won't win."

Seemingly relieved, Tinsley jumped up and we danced for the rest of the night.

CHAPTER 17

The Meeting (Maya)

It was 10:00 a.m. Saturday morning, and the weather was beautiful as I drove to the local coffee shop. Still in shock about how fast the spring went by, I silently looked forward to taking out all my summer and fall clothes that had been pushed to the back of my closet. Parking my mother's BMW next to a motorcycle, I hopped out the car with briefcase in hand, ready to hear my potential client's story. A text message I'd received just minutes earlier indicated that Vince and Damien were already seated.

Scanning the busy café, my eyes landed on Vince. Yet, it was the person sitting next to him that caused me to jump. Hadn't I seen this man before? A worker scurried past me with a mop and bucket in hand. Before I knew what was happening, my briefcase hit the edge of the bucket, causing the water to splatter everywhere, including on nearby customers.

"Dammit," the employee muttered. Before I

could ask if I could help, the disgruntled woman shooed me away. Standing up from my crouched position, I faced the gentlemen who I was meeting again. While Vince looked concerned, Damien looked amused. Still shocked by my reaction to the young ball player, I straightened up and walked over to their table. After a brief hug to Vince, and an awkward handshake to Damien, I sat my bag down next to the empty chair and slid in. Taking a sip from the cup of coffee that Vince ordered for me, it was finally time to get down to business. With nerves intact, I went straight into legal mode.

"So tell me about yourself, Mr. Roseland. I'm not a huge sports fan, so I'm not too familiar with your story."

"You can just call me Damien," he said with a charming smile. "Anyway, there's not much to tell. I was raised in Richmond, Virginia where I also went to college and played ball. Then I got drafted three years ago to the New York Knights. The team owner never really liked me, so the organization as a whole eventually decided to get rid of me. Anyway, I was picked up by the Cougars recently."

As I took out my pen and started writing notes, I couldn't help but be relieved at how well Damien spoke. One of the things that bothered me the most about some athletes was that they were great on the court or the field, but when they got in front of a microphone for an interview, they didn't always sound articulate, educated, or professional.

"What about your family life, do you have any siblings or close cousins?"

Immediately, Damien's body stiffened as he simply shook his head.

"Well," I continued, not easily deterred. "Who raised you?"

"The streets raised me at first. Then I was adopted. My mom is all I have and all I want, honestly."

"Tell me something many people don't know about you, Damien."

Sitting quietly, observing the conversation happening between his client and attorney, Vince was absorbed in the dialogue.

"I went to juvie when I was younger for selling drugs," he admitted while fidgeting with his mustache. "I was there for a couple years, but that was fine with me. It beat living with a foster mother who beat my ass every day. When I got out, I was adopted."

At a loss for words, I took another sip of my beverage and wrote quietly on my legal pad. Realizing that Damien was shutting down, I decided to save the personal life conversation for another day. Instead, I asked the question that I, and thousands of others, really wanted to know.

"Did you rape Janet Springer?"

Looking me dead in my eyes for the first time since I sat down, he said, "No."

"Where were you the night that she was raped?"

An uncertain look came to his face before he smiled and admitted, "I was with Janet, giving her a little bit of big daddy. But she wanted it, it wasn't forced."

Disgusted by his cockiness, I slammed my pen down and began to leave. Standing up, I glanced at Vince and said, "I'm not sure if your client knows how much trouble he's in, but when he realizes he's about five seconds from somebody's prison cell and is ready for some help, tell him to call me."

Sauntering off in my heels, I busted through the front door and headed back to the car. "I could have stayed home for all this shit," I muttered to myself."

Before I could make it to the sports car, a rough hand grabbed my shoulder and forced me to turn around. When I met Damien's eyes, the initial shaky feeling I got, returned.

"I need help, Attorney Kincaid, and I hear you're one of the best. Please help me."

Still unsure of how to proceed, my gut told me to take the case. After a moment of fighting myself, I finally made a decision.

"Ok, Mr. Roseland, I will represent you. But let me tell you this now, you will follow my rules or I will drop your ass. I will be in touch with you after my vacation."

With that, I slid behind the wheel, started the

engine, and peeled out of the parking spot, headed back to my parents' house. Something told me, this was going to be a long and interesting case.

CHAPTER 18

Memory Lane (Damien)

I watched my new attorney race out of the parking lot and then I fell into deep thought. The conversation about my childhood had triggered something inside of me. It was a mixture of anger and sadness. Thinking back to my last foster mother almost made me want to punch out a window of the small coffee shop.

"You ain't shit, and you'll never be shit. How dare you steal money from my damn pocket book!" she yelled while standing over top of me, with spit flying out of her mouth and onto my face. "I should have left your bad ass where I found you. On the street!"

As I began to plead my case, I noticed she had a switch in her right hand. Before I could react, I felt the long whip against my back. Yelping out in pain, my little body trembled in fear. This was my reality. At twelve years-old I was the youngest of all my foster siblings, and oftentimes it seemed like I was also the most hated. What's weird is that, usually, the youngest child gets special treatment, but that definitely wasn't the case in my house, or any temporary residence I lived in. With tears streaming down my face, I noticed my foster sister Caroline crouching in the corner, giggling up a storm. She watched me get beat and flashed a wad of money, which I assumed was from Fran's, my foster mother's, purse. Too hurt and sad to tell on her, I curled up in a fetal position and continued to be verbally abused by the woman whom I was forced to call mom. She was a small woman, weighing only about 115-pounds, but to me, she seemed like a giant. Towering over me, yelling obscenities, I tried to shield my face from her hits.

Kicking me in the stomach while I lay sprawled out on the floor of my living room, Fran continued to berate and scold me for something I didn't even do. Leaving me to cry out in pain, I asked God for what seemed like the millionth time, why He had to let me live in this torture. Tired of beating me, she picked up a lighter on the nearby table, stood, and lit a cigarette. With an evil smirk, she burnt the end of her cigarette on my bare skin. As I was crying out in pain, she gave me one more look before turning in the opposite direction to head into her room. As soon as she disappeared, I ran out the front door. With blurry eyes and a hurt heart, I headed to the neighborhood basketball courts. Grabbing onto the fence, I jumped it and watched the older boys play a quick pickup game.

"Baby," a gentle voice called from behind me. "What's got you feeling down?"

Looking up from the game, my eyes connected with the older woman whom we all called the neighborhood mother, Mrs. Mary Roseland. Standing confident and tall, she looked good for her age. Almost like she was really in her late forties. It was her mission to look after the kids in our area, especially after a drunk driver killed her son and husband. Ever since then she made it her business to reach out and help the youth in the hood. This was admirable, because instead of being angry and blaming the boy who'd killed her family, she simply prayed for him and went around to different schools in Virginia, educating students on the consequences of drunk driving. For me personally, she was always the lady who would feed me when she noticed I wasn't being fed at home, and even bought clothes for me when the holes in my shoes and shirts became noticeable. In short, I loved her.

Slowly, I faced her and allowed her to see the bruises that decorated my face. Finally, I lifted my arm so that she could see my burn. No words were spoken, but the look of sadness that crossed her face as she knelt before me could not be missed. Grabbing me into a bear hug, she held me as I cried all of my hurt and pain onto her shoulders. A week later, I was busted for slinging dope and was put into a juvenile detention center.

The whole time, Mrs. Roseland stood beside me, praying and staying positive. When I was released two years later, she adopted me. For the first time, I was with someone who really loved me.

"You good man?" Vince asked as he walked up to me. Shaking off my thoughts, I nodded.

"Yeah, man. She said she would represent me," I smiled. "She seems so familiar though. At first, I thought she was a chick I used to kick it with or something. She's bad as hell."

Laughing at my rambling, Vince threw his arm over my shoulder and said, "Well, that's all me, young boy. Don't even try to get with her. Matter of fact, I'm staying an extra day out here. I want to surprise her with a nice date later."

After shaking hands, and exchanging a few last words, we hopped into our separate cars. I had to head back to Washington so I could work out on my own before the team began practicing together. I needed to get focused on work so I decided to let my agent and new attorney take care of the rest.

CHAPTER 19

Meet the Kincaid's (Maya)

By noon, I pulled up through the guard shack and gained access to my parent's property. For a second, I marveled at the landscaping around our mansion. It was so beautiful. When my parents first moved to the Hamptons from Prince George's County, Maryland, the wealthiest African-American county in America, I was skeptical about the estate being too showy. For the longest, I thought only snobby people, like my mother's side of the family, lived in the area. But in the five years since they moved in, the place had begun feeling like a second home.

As soon as I parked my car in the five-car garage, my phone went off. Before I could say hello, Vince's voice on the other end filled the air with a boom. While he spoke, I hopped out the car and walked towards the front of the house.

"What do you think about me taking you to a jazz club tonight as a second date and a thank you for taking on Damien's case?"

Quietly placing the key in the door, I turned the knob and was greeted by my mother, who held Brockman in her arms, as usual. I loved my parents with everything in me, but I could only deal with my mom in doses.

"Sure," I responded. "What time can you pick me up?"

"Who is that dear?"mother asked.

"My friend, Vince."

"Oooooh a date!" She clapped so hard that she dropped poor Brockman on the floor. "What time?"

Laughing on the other end, Vince and I set a time. With his voice being so deep, it's no wonder my mom could hear him through the phone.

"Great! We can't wait to meet him. I'll make sure your father is free when Vince arrives."

I watched my mother skip up the stairs with the dog trailing at her feet. I gave a sigh. Turning back to my conversation with Vince, all I could say was, "I hope you're ready to meet the one and only Victoria Kincaid."

***

"Maya!" Ms. Mildred yelled from downstairs.

"Your friend, Vincent, is here for you."

"Coming!" After I made sure my diamond studs were placed perfectly in my earlobes, I walked down the steps and followed the voices. Somehow, my family had already lured Vince into the room where they host all their friends and socials. Walking inside, I noticed the room had been set-up for his arrival. *How embarrassing*, I thought to myself. They were so pressed for me to get married that they were probably scaring Vince off and it was only our second date. Standing up from his chair, which was right across from my parents, he greeted me with a peck on the cheek and handed me a beautiful bouquet of Sunflowers.

"You look beautiful," he began.

"Thank you."

"Ms. Milly, can you take those from Maya and put them in a vase?" Daddy asked.

Once the flowers were taken and I was settled in the seat next to Vince, the interrogation began.

"Where are you from and what do you do?" my mother inquired.

"I'm originally from New Jersey. I went to college on a basketball scholarship and was drafted my sophomore year. I got banged up pretty bad on the court my fourth year in the NBA so I had to retire early. Now, I'm a sports agent."

Nodding slowly, my mother was undoubtedly checking to make sure Vince met her strict standards.

"Do you have any baby mother's that we should know about? I know you athlete types keep those girls on the side. What do they call them nowadays? Sideline whores?"

Ah shit, I thought to myself. *Here we go.* I could always count on my mom to ask whatever the hell was on her mind. Thankfully, Vince had a sense of humor and laughed the question off. "No, ma'am, I do not. In the past, I worked entirely too much to really date or have a relationship." Looking at me for a second, he continued. "I've always said it would take the right woman to come around for me to place work second. I'm really enjoying getting to know Maya."

Sensing my discomfort, my dad re-directed the conversation to a lighter topic. Reaching for his cup of coffee, he began. "So, son, who are some people you've had the chance to represent? Do you cover all sports? I'm a football kind of guy myself."

Smiling at the more exciting subject, Vince visibly relaxed and nodded anxiously to my dad.

"I do. Actually, I've worked with the William's sisters and Kaepernick. My biggest client right now is, Damien Roseland."

In mid-sip, Judge Kincaid almost spit out the coffee in his mouth. Next to him, my mother noticeably sat up straighter, as if she'd seen a ghost. Not realizing their reactions, Vince continued. "In fact, your lovely daughter here is helping me with a legal matter pertaining to Damien right now."

"Are you talking about the rape situation that we've been seeing blasted all over television? He looks guilty to me. Maya, you specialize in civil rights law, honey what on earth can you do for a rapist!"

Hearing the alarm in her voice, Brockman bounded into the room and ran straight into her arms.

"He did not rape her, Mom, that's why I decided to take this case. He's innocent, I met with him, and I have a good feeling about this."

"Sweetheart, let's let these kids go on their date," Dad interrupted."I'm sure Maya knows what she's doing. Representing Damien Roseland could be great for her career."

As we stood up to go, Brockman climbed off my mother's lap and headed straight for Vince, growling and showing his teeth. *He never does this*, I thought. What was up with everybody tonight? After snatching Brockman from Vince's pant leg, we were finally off.

"See you both later. Love you."

CHAPTER 20

Jazz and Things (Vince)

The dance floor was crowded with couples, but we, without a doubt, had the best moves. Well, I did, at least. Maya wasn't much of a dancer, but she looked like she was having a great time, which made me happy. When the song finally ended, I led her back to our table. Sliding back into my chair, I looked over at the woman who was slowly winning me over. Looking back at me, she smiled and placed her hand on top of mine. Gently I reached over and traced a finger along her face. Her cheekbones were beautiful and so well defined. Her lips were as smooth and soft as they come. She was beautiful, which was evident by all the stares she received from the men in the jazz club. I was proud to have her by my side. For a few seconds I took in the sight before me. She had curves for days, class that spoke volumes, and great taste in clothes. Her outfits always seemed to be made just for her. Judging by the amount of money her people had,

I wouldn't have been surprised if they were. The band ended their set and was preparing to take a break. Now was the time that I could really get to know more about Maya.

"Tell me about your childhood," I began. "There are so many things I want to learn about you."

"Well, I've had a pretty complex life." She paused as if debating her next words. "I was adopted when my parents died. I was seven when they passed away. I still have dreams about my birth mother though; she was such a beautiful woman. My sperm donor, on the other hand, wasn't."

She seemed to shudder at the mere mention of her biological father. For a second, Maya looked out into space, like she was holding on to a memory.

"Wow I didn't know. You seem so natural with the Kincaid's," I said, surprised that they weren't her real parents.

"Of course," she continued. "They're my parents and I love them to death. Besides my late grandmother and close friends, they're the closest to me. They can be a pain sometimes, but I love how they challenge me and have high expectations. I don't care much for my mother's side of the family, but my father's side is the best."

"Why is that Maya?"

She let a soft chuckle come out before she

answered. "Mom is from old money so her family looks down on me and my dad. They call me an orphan child behind my back and have always said my father wasn't good enough for my mother to marry since he's more new money. It's really stupid. Love is love to me. Old money, new money, no money at all."

Catching her discomfort, I decided to shift the conversation. "So, thanks again for helping out Damien," I began.

"If you thank me one more time I'm going to hurt you," she said, laughing. "No, but really. He seems like a nice guy who just got caught up in a bad situation. It's funny that he's from Richmond; I lived there before I was adopted. I know how rough some of the areas out there are."

A look of disgust crossed my face. "You actually believe that he's innocent?" I asked.

"Of course, I wouldn't represent him if I didn't think that. Wait, you think he did it?" A look of caution passed over her before I figured I might have said too much. At that moment, I questioned whether it was wise to get Maya involved with the case. If she was so confident of Damien's innocence then that could pose a problem down the line.

"Well, he's done his dirt in the past, but I hope he didn't do this."

Luckily, the band came back to the stage to begin their next set.

"Let's go lady, I want another dance."

Swooping her into my arms, I held her like I'd known her for years. "I talked about myself this whole date," she whispered in my ear. "Next time, it's all about you."

Brushing her comment off, I spun her around so she couldn't see my face. The less she knew about me, the better things would be as far as I was concerned. With her back turned against me, a face popped into my brain. A chill ran down my spine because I knew if things didn't turn out right, I would be screwed.

CHAPTER 21

Truth Hurts (Maya)

Waking up was so peaceful. Though I got up earlier than usual, I felt energized and ready to exercise. Searching for my workout clothes, I threw them on and got ready to head to the gym, which was located just downstairs in my parents' basement. Opening the door of my room, I was greeted by an empty hallway, but heard voices coming from my mothers' quarters. Quietly making my way across the soft carpet, I made sure not to make a sound. I listened from outside her office, with my ear pressed to the door. Usually she only occupied the space when organizing or planning her charity and fundraising events, but something told me that she was in there for a different reason this time.

"She's a grown woman now, Victoria, it's time we tell her!"

"Why?" my mother asked in disgust. "He's a convict."

Hesitant about interrupting, I knocked softly

and pushed open the door, causing both of my parents to jump upright in their chairs. Quickly gathering herself, motioned for me to come inside.

"Maya, darling," she drawled. "Why are you up so early? You're on vacation."

Something told me I had walked in on something I wasn't supposed to hear. Pushing those thoughts to the back of my mind, I explained my desire to get back in shape.

"Why are you guys so tense?" I asked when I noticed my dad's stern expression and mother's nervous half-smile.

Scratching his peppered beard, I watched as my dad leaned back in the leather recliner and stared into space. Finally, with his elbows on the arms of the chair, he leaned forward and gave me an intense gaze before telling me to have a seat in the vacant spot next to him and across from my mother.

"Maya," he began. "When your mother and I adopted you, it was the greatest moment of our lives. You were and still are beautiful, intelligent, and the most caring daughter we could have ever asked for. With that being said, unfortunately, we haven't been totally honest with you."

Sitting silently with Brockman in her lap, mother refused to look up at me.

"Yes. It's true when we adopted you that none of your relatives were reported to be alive. We were given all the names of your immediate family for research purposes and everyone was listed as deceased. Anyway, about nine years ago, while I was speaking with Judge Holloway, you remember the Judge I introduced you to who works out of Virginia?"

With a slight nod from me, he continued. "Well, he mentioned a case involving a young man by the name of Christopher D. Jackson Jr., who was arrested for selling drugs."

Noting my shocked expression at the mention of my late brother's name, he continued his story in an unsteady voice.

"The boy was thrown into a juvenile detention center for two years for something involving drugs. Maya, we want you to know that your brother is alive today. I did my own research and found out he had multiple seizures as a baby, including the one he had the day your parents died. At the hospital, he was pronounced dead, but shortly after, he began breathing again on his own. He was eventually stable enough to be released and was then put into foster care."

Shock took over my body at the mention of my younger brother. "Well, where is he now? I would like to meet him," I asked between clenched teeth. The anger I felt was slowly brewing inside of me and my hands were shaking uncontrollably. They'd been lying to me for years, and I was mad as hell. Taking a deep breath, my mother finally looked up and joined the conversation.

"Honey, we've kept up with his whereabouts

over the years since finding out he was alive," she said. "When Christopher got out of the detention center he was adopted by a Mrs. Roseland, who believed he had potential to be great, despite his rough upbringing. Since then, Christopher has changed his name. He didn't want to be named after the man who killed his mother so he dropped the junior. He now goes by his middle name, Damien, and her last name Roseland. Your new client…"

"Is my brother," I whispered.

Standing up, mother walked around the desk and tried to hug me, but I leaned away and simply stared at her. Did she really expect me to embrace her after receiving this information? After several seconds of watching her outstretched arms, I jumped up from my seat and walked to my room in disgust, while completely ignoring their pleas for me to stay and talk things through with them. Sitting on my bed, I couldn't help but giggle at the situation. What started out as a chuckle turned into a full-blown laugh as I fell to the floor clutching my side. No, I didn't actually think the situation was funny, but the phrase *laugh to keep from crying* came to mind. All these years they'd held this information from me and now when I was defending the guy, they wanted to come clean. Packing my bags, I realized my vacation would be cut short and that I needed to get back to my own home.

PART II

CHAPTER 22

The Workout (Damien)

Sweat poured down my face after I finished, what felt like, the hardest workout of my life.

"Good job today, Roseland," Assistant Coach Griffin said while gripping my shoulder. "This is gonna be one hell of a season for you and the team. Just try to keep those nasty rumors down."

Drinking from my water bottle and still out of breath, I could only manage a half grin and head nod. Coach stared at me for a minute before finally walking back to speak with the other coaches and players. The word rapist had stuck in my head throughout the whole practice, making me angry. The mere thought of my pending case made me practice today like my life depended on it. I loved Janet, and would never hurt her. For ninety minutes straight I thought about what would make her lie like this. The only sane answer seemed to be, to boost her career. It seemed like after the Rihanna and Chris Brown incident, Rihanna became a household name, so maybe Janet was looking for a similar result.

Walking into the locker room, I ignored the conversations happening around me. This was a new team. Though I'd played with many of the guys before, since college, I still hadn't befriended anyone. With a towel wrapped around my waist, I prepared to jump in the shower. Turning around to head to the stalls, Sherrod Brown stepped up to me to dap me up.

"Yo, man, come out with us this weekend. It's my birthday and we're going to celebrate at Stadium. You down?"

Eager to get along with my new teammates, this was a no brainer. "Of course, I'm in, man."

"Cool, I'll send you the details on where to meet and what time."

Dapping him up once again, I grabbed my shower materials and walked to my stall. *This should be fun, I thought. At least it'll get my mind off all the bullshit going on in my life.*

CHAPTER 23

District of Columbia (Maya)

While driving home, silence hung in the air after I told Ivey and Taylor about my supposed vacation to the Hamptons. Since Ivey was now in California, I decided a three-way call would be best for us to have.

"So let me get this shit straight," Taye started. "Your drug addict friend Tinsley wants a life change, you're taking on a case involving some young thug, and that thug happens to be your brother?"

More silence came as my two friends digested the news.

"When do you plan on telling Damien?"Ivey asked in a low voice. She was on set and didn't want to divulge the contents of our conversation to those passing by.

"Honestly, not for a while. I want to do some more work on Damien's case first. He's so stressed with everything else that's going on and I really don't want to add more drama to his life."

Pulling up in front of my place, I told my girls that I would hit them up later, and disconnected the call. After locking my car doors, I walked into my house, left my suitcase by the spiral staircase, and headed straight for my wine cellar. Kicking off my boots, I took my newly filled glass and walked into my office. Powering on my computer, I grabbed a notepad and pen from my desk and began researching Damien Roseland. Articles surfaced that highlighted his stats and career, but what I found most interesting was the charity work he did in inner city communities. He was listed as a mentor and investor in various non-profit organizations. In many interviews, he mentioned wanting to adopt children from situations similar to his and he even had an organization called *The Rose Foundation: Helping Children Everywhere*.

To me, this did not seem like a man who would rape someone. Scrolling through the Google pages, I saw one brief article highlighting his short stint in a Juvenile Detention Center. Photos of Damien and his adopted mother illuminated my screen, and I even caught a few of Damien with Janet. *She seems really close to him in this photo,* I thought to myself. As I enlarged the image, I couldn't help but notice the look of love Janet gave Damien as he grabbed her around the waist. The photo was taken the night of the party, when Janet cried rape. Jotting down notes on my pad, I began to think of different motives that she could have for lying on Damien. She was a fairly well known actress, but maybe she needed more publicity. Maybe she caught wind of Damien being with another woman and became jealous. All of these were potential reasons for lying on him. Pushing my body against the back of my chair, I took another sip of wine and became lost in thought. The way Janet looked at Damien in this picture, reminded me of how Josh used to look at me. Memories like that still came to me sometimes.

Prom Time

"Mother! Where's your diamond necklace that you said I could wear?" I nervously asked while drumming my fingers across the staircase banister after yelling down the steps to my mother.

"Check in my jewelry box," she finally replied after several seconds. Running to grab the piece of jewelry, I heard the doorbell ring. Great, he's here, I silently thought. Hearing my mom gush over my prom date was enough to make me rush to clasp the eye-catching diamond necklace around my neck and straighten my dress. For a second, I glanced in my mother's full-length vanity mirror to admire my look for the night.

In a strapless black Valentino number, with a designer clutch and Lauraine Schwartz jewels, I knew I would be the best-looking girl at the dance. Flashing my million-dollar smile coated with red Dior lipstick, I quickly turned on my new heels and fled back to the stairway. All talk ceased as I appeared at the top of the stairs. At a loss for words, Josh, my date and longtime boyfriend, licked his lips before presenting me with a bouquet of flowers.

"You look beautiful babe..."

Before he could continue, his parents, Mr. and Mrs. Thomas, bounded through the front door with excitement. "You look beautiful, Maya!" Josh's mother exclaimed.

Finally chiming in, my mother agreed.

"They both look great, Tammy. Let's take a few pictures and send them off."

After the photos were taken, our two families walked with us to the driveway. Before I could rescue Josh, I noticed my father yoking him up in a corner.

"Remember, that shotgun I told you I keep in my closet?" I heard my father ask. "Well, it's still there."

Luckily, Mr. Thomas was too caught up in a conversation to notice my dad threatening his son. Walking up to the two of them, I grabbed my date, kissed my father's cheek, and headed to our ride. With a smooth touch, Josh removed the pink corsage from a white box and gently settled it on my wrist. Tonight was going to be special, I thought to myself. Josh grabbed my hand and led me to his rented Aston Martin. We figured having a driver would get in our way after the dance, so we settled for driving ourselves. R&B music played on the radio during the whole fifteen-minute drive, and I felt like I had gone to heaven. Dancing in his arms that night felt like magic. As he tightened his grip around my body, I leaned into his chest, inhaling the scent of his crisp cologne. I was only eighteen but I was so much in love that I knew this was the real deal. Looking up at his baby face, he looked back down to me and softly kissed my forehead. With my eyes closed, I tried to memorize every step and movement. I moved along to the words and beat of the song while wishing for time to just stand still. I didn't get my wish, and the last song of the night finally came to an end.

Hugging me moments later, I was ready for our next stop. Months ago, I had decided to lose my virginity to Josh on the night of prom, and he promised to make the experience special. Leading me through the front doors of the school gym, hand-in-hand we said our goodbyes to all of our friends, including Ivey and Tinsley, and hopped back in the car to head in the direction of the mystery spot. My nerves were all over the place as I waited anxiously to get to the location.

After driving for close to an hour, we arrived at our destination. Handing his keys to the valet at the front, he ran to the passenger side to open my door. Getting out of the car, a sea of black clouded my vision as Josh placed a blindfold over my eyes. With only his hand to guide my path, I let him lead me through the hotel lobby.

I listened while he pressed the entry card against the scanner and pushed open the door.

I was greeted with a cinnamon scent and oldies but goodies songs playing in the background. We were young, but he knew how much I loved that style of music, thanks to my late mama. Finally taking off my blindfold, Josh turned me to face him, and simply said, "I love you" That. night I lost my virginity to the only man I'd ever fully given my heart to, outside of my father, of course.

Before I could get to the end of my daydream, I jumped up to get ready for bed. Standing in the shower, I cried for the loss of my family and for the end of my relationship to my first love. I cried for Damien, because though I'd lived a life of luxury, he'd clearly suffered. I know I hadn't done anything wrong, but in my heart, I hoped he could forgive me for leaving him that night in the hospital. Mama had always told me to look after him, and I didn't live up to her request.

CHAPTER 24

New Friends (Maya)

NBA STAR DAMIEN ROSELAND SEEN
VISITING LOCAL STRIP CLUB LAST
WEEKEND WITH TEAMMATES JUST
WEEKS AFTER BEING NAMED PRIMARY
SUSPECT IN THE RAPE CASE OF ACTRESS
JANET SPRINGER

I was in the middle of ordering Chinese food when I heard the news report, but quickly slammed my phone down and walked calmly towards the TV in my office to turn up the volume. As I watched the clip of Damien throwing money at the local strippers, sliding crisp bills through the cracks of their asses, as if he were on the set of Nelly's video *Tip Drill*, the door to my office banged open and my assistant ran to my side.

"Attorney Kincaid, I just saw the clip online," Annette said with concern etched on her face. "Anything I can do?"

"Please call me a car. I need to go visit Mr. Roseland."

Rushing to fulfill my requests, Annette returned shortly to let me know that my car was having mechanical issues and it would take at least an hour to be fixed. I didn't have that kind of time.

"Okay, never mind, I'll just metro it. Hailing a cab may take too long, especially now that it's lunchtime."

Taking off my heels, I slipped into a pair of Tory Burch flats that I kept under my desk. Damien's practice facility was just off the red line, which wasn't too far of a ride from my office. Annette looked on in fascination. In the three years that she'd been my assistant she could count on one hand the amount of times her boss had taken public transportation.

"What?" I asked, noticing her looking at me. Ignoring my question, she smiled and left the room.

While waiting for fifteen-minutes in the Foggy Bottom Metro Station, I was bombarded with calls and texts. Didn't these people know that I wasn't going to speak with them yet? After getting off the phone with my dad to update him about all that was going on, I turned off my device and boarded the train to get settled in my seat. Thoughts of the conversation I had with my parent's just days ago came to mind. I was still pissed off that they had lied to me, but was happy I forgave them. At the end of the day, I needed them. Before I knew it, I was staring out of my window wondering if I could really move forward and handle this case. I heard a gentleman's voice, snapping me back into reality.

"Ma'am I'm sorry to bother you but I couldn't help but notice you when I first got on the train."

With an attitude, I noted his reflection in the window and turned my attention to the unwanted visitor. I was pleasantly surprised when I was greeted with a deep stare from a brother dressed immaculately in a charcoal suit who was standing next to my seat. *Good taste*, I thought to myself. Before I could respond, Mr. suit-and-tie continued.

"I wanted to congratulate you on winning that case with the mother earlier this year. I've read enough about you and have seen you enough on television to know what a great attorney you are."

As he spoke, I found myself mesmerized by his piercing eyes and handsome features, but a quick thought about Vince made me jump back to reality.

"Thank you sir, I appreciate it. I'm Maya Kincaid and you are..."

As if remembering his manners, his hand shot towards me. Shaking my hand he responded, "I'm Corey Townsend, a retired FBI detective. I just moved here from New York."

"Good stuff," I replied. "What brought you to this area?"

Just then, the train stopped in the tunnel as the conductor announced that the cars in front of us were backed up. Ignoring the announcement, the fine former detective answered my question.

Motioning for him to take the seat next to me, our conversation continued.

"Once I retired, I decided to start my own private investigation company, so I'm setting up shop down here. My new offices are right here in the city. But enough about me, I want to hear all the great things you have going on right now."

Confused about where this was going, I didn't respond, and instead, waited for him to finish explaining.

"I'm referring to the Janet Springer case."

With an eyebrow raised, I sat quietly for a moment, thinking about my next words.

"So," I began. "Do you think Damien is guilty as well?"

"If I based my opinion on what the news is reporting, then I would said yes; however, there are still a lot of questions that need to be answered. As of now, I honestly can't say."

"Even if you wanted to, you wouldn't say though," I said with a small smile.

"That too, I wouldn't want to offend you," he laughed.

The train began moving again and we were approaching my stop.

"Well how about this?" I said. "Let's keep in touch. Since you're an outsider I would love to pick your brain about the details of this case."

After reaching into my sorority engraved cardholder for my business card, I took out my pen and wrote my personal number on the back of it.

"Is that your way of getting rid of me?"

With a sincere smile, I simply said, "If I wanted to get rid of you I would have done so ten minutes ago. Here, take my card."

"I'll be sure to stay in contact." He paused as if choosing his next words carefully. "And maybe we can even do dinner sometime."

With that, Corey tucked my card inside his pocket, and moved to the side so I could get out of the seat. Facing towards the sliding doors, I glanced back once more, catching the investigator looking me up and down. I delivered a smirk before finally exiting the train.

CHAPTER 25

No Idle Threats (Damien)

"And that's all for today," Coach Taylor yelled.

Slowly, I walked off the court and headed to the sideline to grab my water bottle.

"We'll meet again, same time and place tomorrow, fellas. Good work today. Hey Roseland, let me talk to you really quick."

My stomach clenched as I anticipated what was about to come. Would I be getting fired? Would Coach tell me pack my bags and go home?

My insides continued to knot up as I walked over to him. Some of my teammates rushed around me to get to the locker room, while others headed back to the court to continue practicing. They all seemed thankful that they wouldn't have to be left alone with such a dominant figure.

"Damien," Coach began, pointing for me to sit on the bench next to him. Uncertain of where he was going with this conversation, I waited for him to keep talking. Breaking into a rare smile,

Coach Taylor grabbed my shoulder and beamed a smile so wide that I was able to count all thirty-two teeth in his mouth.

"Only a few weeks in, and you're kicking ass, man. One thing I would highly recommend though, is to work on that jump shot. Other than that..."

It took a couple of seconds for it to sink in that I wasn't getting booted off the team, but once my mind recognized his words, a deep sigh of relief was released and I took in every word that one of the top NBA coaches of all time was telling me.

Once the Preseason comes around, you'll be ready for show time."

"Thanks, Coach," I replied with a small grin. Inside, my heart was beating like crazy.

Snapping back into his role, Coach Taylor stood up with a serious look, grabbed my shoulder, and leaned me into him while eyeing the cameras that surrounded us.

"With all that said, please don't give me a reason to kick you off this team. First, the alleged rape, and now your strip club shenanigans."

Pausing for a brief second, Coach looked me dead in the eye and said, "Get this shit under control, and now. I have the NBA Commissioner looking at me, telling me to get everything taken care of. The public wants us to release you even before the trial starts. I know the Knights dropped you and I would hate to do the same."

Nodding my head in understanding, I shook

Coach's hand and ran to join my teammates, who were still on the court shooting around. Practice was over but I was just revving up.

CHAPTER 26

Ground Rules (Maya)

Finally arriving at the practice facility, I followed the sound of basketballs and people's voices. After passing through security, I stood courtside and watched in fascination as Damien expertly dribbled the ball and passed it off to his teammates. Practice was over but he was so focused that he didn't pay attention to the nearby cameras or me. I was surprised that members of different news stations were even allowed inside the arena during the team practice, but Damien didn't seem the least bit bothered. A couple of reporters approached me, but I wasn't interested in speaking with them. I was more concerned about getting Damien under control. Finally, the extra practice session ended and Damien ran off the court and in my direction.

"I didn't think you noticed I was here," I said when he reached my side.

"Everyone noticed you. You came in here looking like you flew off the pages of some high fashion or business magazine. Plus, you had that angry black woman look on your face. I'm sure I know why, too," he said while side eyeing the cameras, which were steadily rolling nearby.

"Go get dressed, we need to go somewhere more private to talk. I hope you drove here, I had to take the metro."

"You took the metro? You really are down for me, huh?" Damien joked before walking towards the locker rooms. Within an hour, he was showered and ready to get down to business.

After placing our orders, we handed the server our menus. The entire time I watched Damien follow the young waitress' ass as she walked away. Clearing my throat, he looked at me and rolled his eyes.

"Tell me what happened, Damien. What were you thinking? Why would you go out to a strip club and act like you were on set for a rap video? In case you forgot, your ass is on the line for rape."

"Attorney Kincaid are you always this tense?"

"Excuse me? I'm surprised you're not tense, seeing that your life is spiraling out of control. Have you even considered the fact that you could be dropped by your team any day now?"

Ignoring my comment, Damien took a sip of his water and picked up his phone. *This is a child I'm dealing with*, I fumed to myself. For several seconds we sat in silence. Damien remained on his phone while I sat back in my seat and examined him. *He shares my cheekbones and eyes*, I thought silently. Yes, we varied in height, but I could see why. Our dad was a tall man, and mom was short, so it made sense.

"Are you going to look at me all day or are you going to go over what you've found so far that will help my case," Damien said, his eyes cast downward, still looking at his phone.

Sucking my teeth, I grabbed a manila folder out of my briefcase and slapped it down on the table. The impact of the action caused Damien to quickly look up.

"Put the phone away and let's get some things straight, Mr. Roseland."

Reluctantly, he stored his phone away before looking at me and waiting for me to continue.

"Before we begin I would like to establish some rules.

    One. You need to stay away from women outside of your charity events.

    Two. No talking to reporters or anyone regarding your case without me present.

    Three. You need to be completely honest with me about everything.

    Four. You will treat me with respect.

    Five. You will not go to any parties or strip clubs until this situation is resolved."

Anger flashed over his eyes. "Who are you to tell me what to do?"

"I'm your lawyer, and the person trying to keep your ass out of jail."

Leaning back into his chair, Damien sighed in resignation and finally agreed to my instructions.

"Great," I clapped. "Now that we have that in order let's go over what I've found so far. Janet may settle with us outside of court, but if she decides not to, we need to be prepared. I've reached out to everyone who attended the party that night and have testimonies from people who say Janet was getting cozy with you the whole time. I even spoke with her good friend, who knew about your relationship and is just as shocked as you are by the allegations.

"In the police report that Janet filed, I noticed something interesting. She admits that this was your first sexual encounter together; then she says that in the beginning she consented to the sex, but later woke up to find you forcefully entering her. Here, read her detailed account."

Handing over the report, I watched Damien's eyebrows bunch together as he digested Janet's details of the night.

I halfway woke up when Damien clamped his hand over my mouth and pinned me down on the bed. He then proceeded to perform anal sex on me then, doggy style. When I tried to resist him, he slapped and punched me. During the attack he kept repeating, "Say I love you Damien" while pulling my head. Afterwards I bled from the vaginal and rectal areas and was in excruciating pain. I went to the doctor later that morning and they used a rape kit to compile information.

After reading her detailed account, Damien placed the paper back into the folder and shook his head. "This is ridiculous," he said. "I would never hurt Janet. I'm a lot of things, but a rapist and woman beater aren't two things that I am."

"I know. This is why I need your version of what happened that night. I know you told me your side of the story before, but I need you to sit back and really reflect on that night. Beginning to end."

For thirty-minutes, I listened to Damien relive the details. Several things stuck out to me, but I decided not to share those thoughts with him. The two biggest questions I had moving forward were: First, Damien left around 2:00 a.m., but Janet says the attack happened around 2:30. Which was it? Which led me to my next and most important question. Who else was in that house? Something was really off about this.

"Can we talk about something else?" Damien asked, interrupting my thoughts.

For a second, I noticed a sad look in his eyes. There were times when he spoke that I wanted to reach over and hug or hold him. It saddened me to know how hard of a life my brother had had, and that he was in this situation.

"Of course we can."

"So," he began. "How's Vince doing?"

The eyes that had been reflecting sadness

suddenly had a twinkle of mischief in them. Oh my God, I thought. He had those same eyes as a little boy when he would break my Barbie's. Ignoring the memory, I pointed my fork at him and told him to mind his business.

"Aww come on, Attorney. Do you like my boy?"

"You can call me Maya when we're not in court or in front of reporters," I told him. "As for Vince, he's becoming a new friend. We'll see how it goes."

For a second, I thought about Vince and how he seemed to think Damien was guilty.

"Are you two really close?" I asked.

"Oh, definitely. He's been with me for a few years, ever since I was twenty and first joined the league. He's like a mentor, and my mom loves him. I admit, sometimes he does come across as creepy though. It's like he's living through me since he never had the chance to finish his basketball career. Even still, I value his friendship and advice."

For some reason *living through me* stuck out about what Damien just said.

"And what about Mrs. Roseland? It's obvious you adore your mother."

Like a kid in a candy shop Damien moved his chair closer to mine and pulled out photos from his wallet of him and his mother together. "She's my everything. A true Angel. If it weren't for her I wouldn't be here right now. I want her to have everything and to be happy."

"Does she live close by?"

"Oh no, she refuses to leave Richmond, but it's okay. That's where home is for her. I purchased her a nice house in a great neighborhood out there. That's why I'm happy about being traded, so I can be closer to her and can see her more often."

For a second, the conversation paused as I debated my next words.

"I'm originally from Richmond," I said softly. "Off of Chamberlayne Avenue, actually."

Stunned by my words, I told Damien to pickup his jaw off the table and we both began laughing.

"Girl, you're from the straight up hood. I lived not too far from there. But I'm confused, don't you come from money? Why were you living in the slums?"

Choosing my words carefully, I motioned for the waitress to bring us the check.

"My family was dysfunctional to say the least. Anyway, eventually I was adopted."

A brief pause settled over the table as we both reflected on our childhoods.

"We have a lot in common," he said. "I can't lie, I'm surprised."

Standing up to prepare to leave, I thought about how he would react if he knew exactly how much we really had in common. As he stood, everyone in the restaurant stared at his six-foot-six frame. Leaning down to loop his arm through mine, he pulled me to the door and said, "Let's go, Richmond homie." Laughing at our newfound bond, I let him lead me to the car. Later on, I made some calls and was able to schedule a much needed meeting in New Jersey for the following Monday.

***

As the driver pulled through the wrought iron gates, I really didn't know how this meeting would go. A secretary met us in the lobby of the law office and ushered Damien and me inside a small meeting area.

"Attorney Carmichael will be with you momentarily." With this, the woman dressed in a head-to-toe black skirt and jacket ensemble stood to the side as we heard footsteps approaching the room. Motioning for Damien to stand with me to greet Janet and her lawyer, I shook hands with them both.

"Nice meeting you, Attorney Kincaid. Now, what can my client and I do for you and Mr. Roseland?"

Seated around the circular table, I looked between Janet and her representative, Attorney Carmichael. Clearing my throat, I figured it was best to communicate directly with Janet. Eyeing the beautiful woman sitting before me, it was easy for me to see why Damien was so enthralled with the actress. She was even more beautiful in person.

"I wanted a chance to speak with Janet about

the allegations she has made against my client."

Gazing intently at the woman, who was around my age, I watched her shift hesitantly in her seat.

"Janet," I began. "We both know Damien did not rape you. Can you tell me what really happened that night?"

"Excuse me," interrupted her white haired attorney, who appeared to be in his late 60's.

"Please do not be insensitive to my client, who has already been through so much since your client decided to take advantage of her."

Crossing my legs under the table, I decided that taking a less aggressive approach would probably be best for this situation.

"According to my client, you two had consensual sex. In fact, you were involved in an actual relationship."

"Why would you do this to me, J?" Damien interjected. For the first time since she'd walked in, Janet gave Damien eye contact. Her look reminded me of sadness, pain, anger, and uncertainty.

Straightening her shoulders, Janet tried to gain some strength before she spoke. "You did this to yourself."

"Look," I continued. "We came here to see how we could settle this outside of court. Is it money you would like, Janet? Attorney Carmichael, how can we handle this best?"

"Can I speak more with Ms. Springer and get back to you both on this?" her attorney asked.

Accepting this, we shook hands and headed back to the car.

"I might as well buy a house in Jersey or New York," I muttered under my breath. This was the second trip I'd made to the area in a month.

"You got the money, why not?" Damien smirked.

Deciding to ignore his sarcastic comment, I pushed open the front doors of the law offices, and was greeted with reporters and paparazzi. Damn, I thought. *I should have known that our visit would be tipped off to the media*. Pushing Damien back into the building, I told him to remain inside while I had the car pulled around. Before leaving, I got the attention of some security guards who agreed to help get Damien out to the car. After sliding them some money for their help, I ran back outside to distract the media. After answering a couple of questions, our black SUV pulled up. On cue, the two guards and Damien came out the door and we made our way through the crowd. Once inside, we quickly hit the automatic locks and the driver sped out of the area.

"Vince said you never worked with celebrities before, but you handled that like a champ," Damien commented when we finally made it out of the throng of hounds. Within fifteen minutes, we were at LaGuardia, ready to catch our flight home.

CHAPTER 27

In the Moment (Maya)

Lightly knocking on his door, I stood back and waited for Vince to let me in. This was my first time at his place. He had invited me over for dinner and I was a little nervous. Before I could knock a second time, the door swung open and I saw him on the other side, looking like he had just won the lottery.

"Hey beautiful," he beamed while stepping aside to let me enter his new apartment, which he'd recently purchased in order to be close to Damien. *Thank God, he's clean*, I thought to myself. But then again he could have just straightened up his place for my visit. Trying to shake any possible negative thoughts out of my head, I smiled and offered him a small kiss.

"I like your home," I said as I looked around. Pictures of him with his family and friends were scattered around the living room. His apartment was nice and appropriate for a man who lived alone. Walking around, I noticed he had set his dining room table for us.

"Awwww isn't this cute," I said jokingly. Blushing back at me, he pointed inside the kitchen. Not only did I smell the scent of macaroni and cheese, collard greens, and corn bread, but I saw Turkey Necks. Turning back to Vince, I couldn't help but be impressed.

"How'd you know I liked turkey necks?" I asked.

"Because you said it the first time we went out, remember?"

I recalled that Ms. Francis would secretly fix me turkey necks when I was growing up. Mother despised soul food and preferred a more upscale meal for her family; therefore, Ms. Francis would sneak me the food she knew I really loved. Vince's dinner tasted as good as it looked and I had to stop myself from licking my fork. After a couple glasses of wine, we were cracking jokes and enjoying our time together. Things took a serious turn when Vince asked me about my last real relationship. With a stone face, I played with my cheesecake instead of answering his question.

"Maya?" he prodded.

Sighing, I placed my spoon down and looked up, until my eyes met his. "Vince, my last real relationship was in college. With a guy named Josh. I've dated since then, but I haven't been able to really let anyone get close to me since him."

"Well, what happened with you two, if you

don't mind me asking?"

Moving hair out of my face, I let my mind go back to the day I caught my long-time boyfriend with someone else. Josh and I had been together for four years, since our junior year of high school. After graduating top of our class, we both decided to attend the same college, with hopes of one day getting married. It wasn't until our third year that things came crumbling down. Staring into my plate I still remembered everything that happened vividly.

After being dismissed from class early one day during spring semester, I decided to head over to Josh's house instead of my own. Later that day I had to meet with the debate team and I was hoping to get some rest before then. In college, I wore many hats, and to say I was stressed was an understatement. I knew Josh would be home and was done with classes for the day. As I turned onto his street, I thought of calling him to let him know I was coming. Instead, I decided to just use my personal key to surprise him. Big mistake. Pulling into a parking spot near the basketball court in his complex, I noticed a familiar silver Nissan Altima parked near the front. Not thinking too much of it, I grabbed my book bag out of the back seat and walked towards his building.

After slipping the key into the lock, I gently turned the doorknob and let myself in. Unfortunately for me, I never made it past the entrance of the apartment as I stared in horror at the scene in front of me. Bent over the coffee table was my Josh. Standing over him was Devin Simmons, our friend and the University's current President of the Student Government Association. They were so into their act, neither of the guys looked up at my arrival. For what seemed to be hours, I watched as the man I loved had sex with someone I had considered a friend, someone who also happened to be a man. Finally, I couldn't take any more.

"You've gotta be fucking kidding me!" I yelled with tears covering my face.

With a quickness, a horrified Devin looked up at me, slid out of Josh, and reached for his khaki's, which lay strewn across the sofa. An ashamed Josh stood up and pleaded with his eyes, "Babe, it's not what you think."

Not giving him a chance to give me a weak explanation, I stormed out the door with disgust written all over my face and tears of sadness falling down my cheeks. After four years, Josh had chosen a man over me. Nothing could describe how I felt in that moment. It felt like I was in the middle of a nightmare.

Now, years later, I still think back to that day and wonder how I missed the signs. Soon after I caught the two of them together, Josh admitted to me that he had been confused for a while. Scared that I would tell someone, Devin wrote me a ten-page letter, expressing his guilt and pleading for me to keep what I saw, a secret. Since we had never had a homosexual SGA President, Devin was shaking at the idea of being ridiculed and of not being taken seriously. Plus he had dreams of running for Senator one day, so he thought his sexuality would affect his chances. Still embarrassed at the cheating scandal, I chose to keep everything to myself anyway. The only people I shared it with were my girls and my parents.

"He cheated," I told Vince.

I could tell he wanted me to explain the details, but thankfully he was kind enough to drop the subject altogether. An uncomfortable silence surrounded us. Unable to take it for any longer, I asked to use the restroom.

"Go straight down the hall and it's the last door on the right."

Rising from my chair, I walked to the bathroom, knowing Vince was watching my every step. Glancing into the mirror, I got my emotions under control while double-checking my hair and teeth. Determined not to let distant memories put a damper on my night, I decided to do a little snooping. Mother always told me that you could tell a lot about a man by how he kept his bathroom and by what he kept in his drawers. Hearing clinking in the kitchen, I knew he was busy cleaning up and wouldn't miss me for very long. After searching every drawer and even the trash can, I found nothing suspicious. With nothing ringing a bell, I closed the cabinet and prepared to exit. Outside the door, I could hear the dishwasher running and Vince moving around in the living room. Turning the water on, I pretended to wash my hands, and finally walked out. My chest caught in my throat when I discovered Vincent waiting for me at the end of the hallway. Still tipsy from the wine I'd downed earlier, I didn't know what was going on.

With music playing in the background and what seemed like thousands of candles flickering throughout the darkened room, my mind traveled to a million different places. Standing in the doorway of his bathroom, I waited as this fine specimen began to walk up to me.

"What are we doing?" I whispered to myself, though it came out, out loud.

"We're doing what you want us to do, Maya."

Still unsure about what would happen next, Vince brought me into his arms, making my knees buckle. Grabbing hold of my hand, he gently led me into his bedroom. Moving my body away from his, he gazed down into my eyes and stared into my pupils with such power that I wanted to look away, yet, I never did. No more words were exchanged for what seemed like hours, until, *You Remind Me of a Jeep* began to play in the background.

"What is this, grown and sexy hour?" I nervously giggled. *I sound so stupid and inexperienced*, I thought silently. Sweeping me up and into his oversized bed, he ignored my inquiry while palming my breasts. Easing my clothes off my body, he sat back and admired my petite body while fingering my tresses. Sprawled across his satin sheets, I stared back.

"I've been into you since the first time I saw you." A few seconds passed before he continued. "Now I want to make love to you in a way that you've never experienced before."

At that moment, all I could do was close my eyes and smile. I took in his cologne and his dominating presence. I was ready for him, and had been ready for a long time. I just prayed that my heart could handle my actions.

"I want you to," I whispered back. I didn't think he heard me, as my words became lost in a sea of passion as he removed my lace underwear and began to thrust his condom- covered Adonis inside of me. Making love to the sounds of R. Kelly, I knew our lives would be forever changed after that night. It was just the beginning.

For the next few weeks, Vince and I were inseparable. We took turns visiting each other's places, and I even brought him with me to my firm's July 4th barbecue. To say everybody loved him was an understatement. It was like he knew the right words to say to anyone who came up to us. During this time, I also became close with Damien. I was determined to become more than just his lawyer; I wanted to ultimately be his friend. With my other clients, I kept things strictly professional, but my other clients weren't my brother, Damien was. We'd been on the phone for a while discussing his case when Damien decided to invite me over to his place.

"Maya! Come visit my spot. You still haven't been out to see it."

On the other end, I smiled so wide that my cheeks hurt. It touched me to know that my baby brother loved spending time with me. I had an actual relationship, great friends, awesome job, and now my family was finally coming together. The only problem was that Damien still didn't know I was family. That realization caused me to sigh into the phone.

"What's wrong?" he asked, visably concerned.

"Oh nothing," I quickly replied. "I'll come through this week, just tell me when and what time."

In my head, I figured now was the best time to let the cat out the bag.

CHAPTER 28

The Estate (Maya)

"Mother, it will be fine," I promised

"Well, you must call me the minute you leave his house. If he gets upset about the news, I don't want him killing you or something."

"He would never hurt me, now bye." Hanging up from my call, I pulled around the circular driveway in Ashburn in amazement. This sprawling mansion made my little condo look like Section 8 housing. Turning the car off, I sat and marveled at the giant fountain running in front of me. Music was coming from the backyard. Damien was probably hosting one of his infamous parties that Vince told me about. I was happy that he was following my rules and not going out. With that being said, if he wanted to party at his home, it was fine by me as long as he was careful. Stepping my newest Manolo Blahnik editions on the cobblestone, I was greeted by a man dressed in all black, wearing sunglasses, who judging by his nametag and badge, was an attendant.

Tossing him the keys to my baby, I pulled my sunglasses off and headed to the front door. Ringing the doorbell, I waited nervously for someone to answer. Today was the day I would be telling Damien the truth.

"If it ain't my sexy ass attorney!" Damien's voice boomed over the music when he threw open the door. Surprised that he, instead of a member of his housekeeping team, had personally greeted me, I stood stunned, with what probably looked like a crazy smile on my face.

Grabbing my hand, he led me on a tour throughout the house with the energy of a child. After a look at his expansive house, which included eight bedrooms and six bathrooms, which I later found out my best friend Taylor had helped him pick out, we finally retreated to his living room to get down to business. Smiling at me, Damien crossed one foot over his knee and thanked me for stopping by. Pushing my nerves to the side, I sat up in what I hoped appeared to be confidence. Clearing my throat, I clasped my hands together at my knee and figured it was now or never. This issue was weighing heavily on my heart.

"Damien," I started. After several seconds, my eyes met his. The eyes that I remembered from our childhood stopped me from making my announcement. Instead, I said something else.

"We're gonna beat this case come hell or high water."

With a smile that could probably be seen from miles away, he swooped me up from the couch and did a jig.

"I already knew that. I have an amazing lawyer. No, seriously, Maya, thank you for working so hard to clear my name. You're God sent."A slight smile came to his face as he continued. "In fact, my mom wants to meet you! Can you come spend a weekend with us?"

Noticing the confused look on my face, he hurried to continue. "Please? She's so excited, and I've told her all about you. You're from Richmond and haven't been back since you left. Don't you want to come with me and see your old neighborhood and everything? It may not seem professional, but for some reason I've become really close to you. You remind me of someone, I think it was someone I grew up with … or something."

His pleading look was all I needed.

"Of course I'll come," I answered with a forced smile. "When do we leave?"

"This Friday, the team has the weekend off. Thanks so much Maya. I'll tell my mom you're coming."

The professional side of me wanted to suggest I get a hotel, but the big sister side wanted to enjoy my brother and learn everything that there was about him. With these thoughts, I simply smiled.

"Sounds good, thanks for the invite."

CHAPTER 29

Richmond (Maya)

Two days later, I was in the car with Damien and on my way to Richmond. *What the hell am I doing?* I asked myself. My mother kept calling but I refused to take her calls. She always knew when I was lying, and I wasn't prepared to tell her about my last minute trip. I stared out the window as Damien drove south on I-95. The sun was beaming bright and the scenery outside was beautiful. Luckily, there wasn't much traffic as we drove down the interstate.

"Is she really that bad?" Damien asked.

"Who?"

"Your mom. I'm far from nosy, but I see she's called you like four times since we got in the car."

A small giggle left me before I turned toward my little brother.

"You may not be nosy, but she is."

Noting my discomfort, Damien turned the conversation around. For the duration of the ride, I learned more about him and his upbringing. To say that he'd lived a tough life was putting it mildly. For three hours, I listened while he reflected on being abused, molested, and tormented as a child. I sat stunned as he told me about being slapped around by his former foster mother. I was in disbelief when he shared tales of having to sell dope and steal, but what hurt me the most was when he opened up about being sexually assaulted by his foster mother's supposed best friend. It was sad to hear all that he had been through.

"I was around nine or ten-years-old when Fran's friend Sheena came over. She would rub on me at first, but soon it became more. Fran often asked Sheena to babysit the others and me. It was during those times that she would remove my pants when the other kids were playing outside, and suck me off. At first I enjoyed it, until she made me return the favor."

Touching his shoulder, I silently encouraged him to continue.

"She pushed my head down between her legs and made me eat her out. It was the worst. She smelled disgusting, and even though I was young, I could tell she was a nasty woman. Long story short, eventually she forced me to have sex with her. A couple months later, after a routine examination at my pediatrician's, it was determined that I had Chlamydia. My foster mom called me all kinds of names. When I told her that Sheena did it to me, she called me a liar and beat my ass."

Before even realizing it, my eyes watered and I couldn't stop the tears from falling. My brother had been through so much, and for some reason I felt responsible.

"What's wrong?" Damien asked while he searched his glove compartment for napkins or tissues.

"Everything you said. No child should ever go through something like that."

As Damien pulled off of an exit, he turned to me briefly and gave a weak smile. "It made me stronger. Now I can help kids in the inner city like me or those in foster care. I spread my message and try to give these kids strength. They have to know that their circumstances don't make their future."

Dabbing my eyes, I noticed we were pulling up into a long paved driveway. The house it led to was beautiful yet not showy. Damien turned off the car as I sat and took in the three-story brick home with four columns lining the outside. I hopped out to get my suitcase, but Damien refused to let me carry anything. Such a man, I thought. Walking up to the front door, the door quickly opened before we could even climb to the top step. A woman with the kindest smile stood with her hands on her wide hips. A worn apron covered the front of her body and I could tell that she'd come straight from the kitchen.

"Damien, get on in here and tell this beautiful attorney of yours to get in here too."

Leaving the door open for us, he led the way with our suitcases. A blush met my cheeks at his mother's compliment. Damien threw our luggage into the entryway and chased his mother into the kitchen and enveloped her in the most loving hug. He loomed over her, kissing her cheeks and squeezing the life out her. She gave a hearty laugh as Damien damn near threw her into the air. "Boy stop." Mrs. Roseland playfully swatted his arm with her hand. I could tell that, despite Damien's stature, she was the real one running the show. Pushing her son to the side, Mrs. Roseland reached out to me.

"Welcome to our home, dear," she beamed.

"Thank you so much for having me. It's good to be back in Richmond."

For a second, Mrs. Roseland searched my eyes, as if she were searching for something. Moments later, she smiled and motioned towards Damien to show me the house and take me up to my room. Mrs. Roseland's house was truly a home. It felt so warm and inviting. Black art hung throughout the place and the furniture took on a family feel. Every room was decorated a different way. According to Damien, the place was built from the ground up. Placing my bags in the guest room, we headed back downstairs to the living room while Mrs. Roseland finished up dinner.

"Mom, you know I can't eat what you're cooking," Damien complained.

"Oh please," she said with a roll of her eyes.

"You're a growing boy and I'm sure one serving of macaroni and cheese won't hurt your body, so sit down and let your mama serve you this good food."

I couldn't help but laugh. Damien wasn't a growing boy, he was grown, but I bit my tongue and admired the mother-son connection that I watched going on before me. With a defeated face, Damien walked to the table and sat down.

"Boy, you have five seconds to get on up and wash those dirty little hands of yours. Plus, you need to wait. I have two guests coming over. Mrs. Oliver, my neighbor, just lost her husband and I know she needs a friend right now. Plus my friend Sherman is coming, too."

A dark look came over Damien. Instead of commenting, he washed his hands and sat in the living room just as the doorbell rang.

"Need me to set the table or do anything, Mrs. Roseland?" I asked, trying to appear helpful.

"No baby, just have a seat with Damien, we'll eat shortly. Thank you for offering. Oh and please just call me Mary."

Rushing toward the door, Mrs. Roseland, or Mary, wiped her hands on the front of her apron and noticeably straightened her wig. Walking to the living room, I sat next to Damien and watched as he studied the tennis game that was playing on television. Something was obviously wrong, and I decided to take the time to stay silent. A deep voice interrupted the commentator's voice and I turned just as an older man placed a kiss on Mary's cheek. In a state of bliss, Mary didn't notice me looking, and continued to giggle like a young schoolgirl. Now, it was making sense. This man was dating Damien's mother and Damien didn't like it. As they came closer to the living room, I noticed Damien stiffen up.

"Damien and Maya, meet my good friend Sherman. Sherman, this is my son Damien and his friend Maya."

I winced at being called Damien's friend. At the end of the day I was still his lawyer and didn't want to appear unprofessional. Brushing off the introduction, I shook hands and said hello. Before Damien could stand and give a greeting, someone else knocked on the door. Mary hurried back to the entry, giving Damien the opportunity to sit back down and divert his attention back to the tennis match. A loud laugh carried through the house as Mary's neighbor came inside. A second round of introductions were made and it was finally time to eat.

I piled my plate high with the delicious soul food. I noticed Mrs. Oliver openly staring at me. There was tension as we all sat around the dining room table, eating. Damien kept looking up at Sherman, while Mrs. Oliver sized me up.

"How long have you two been dating, Maya?"

Damien smirked, while I damn near choked on my chicken wing. If she only knew.

"Mrs. Oliver, Damien and I work together.

I'm originally from Richmond so he invited me to come down for a couple days since I haven't been back down here in years."

Nodding slowly, the older woman with gray hair turned back to her food. Silence followed as Damien cleared his throat and glanced back at Sherman.

"Baby, Mr. Sherman here runs a literacy program right here in Richmond for high school students. You should meet with the group of young folks and help out one of these days, once you get some free time."

"Cool."

Ashamed at how rude Damien was acting, I joined in the conversation.

"Mr. Sherman that sounds great! Damien works with Reading Recharged now, so he has experience with children and trying to increase literacy in the inner city."

Hesitantly Sherman responded. "That would be great. We could always use some help whenever you're in town."

Damien grunted and went back to his plate.

"How old are you, Maya? Sorry for prying, but you seem so familiar."

"I just turned twenty-nine not too long ago."

Nodding again, she continued. "What about your family, what are your parents' names? Since you're from here, maybe that's how I know you."

Sitting up in my chair, I wanted to reach across the table and strangle this woman for trying to poke her nose in my business.

"My parents died when I was younger."

"I'm sorry to hear that," she said. "I know losing someone you love is hard. My husband recently passed away from prostate cancer. Plus, I'm a nurse and I've seen many people leave us under different circumstances. It's been a hard job but I still go back after all these years. You know, when I first got here I thought you and Damien were together. Call me a prying old woman if you will, but there's chemistry between you two. If I didn't know any better I would think you guys were related."

Silence followed her comment and for a couple for seconds she stared at me with a look of familiarity.

"Well, who's ready for dessert?" Mary asked.

As she jumped up to grab her homemade cheesecake, Damien excused himself and went to his room. For the next twenty minutes, the conversation lightened up as we talked about current events, politics, and entertainment. With Damien out of sight, Mary gazed more openly at Mr. Sherman, laughed loudly at his jokes, and would touch him occasionally. It was a look of someone in love. The night came to a close and I decided to wash the dishes as Mary showed her other two guests out. Once the last dish was washed and dried, Mary came back and shook her head.

"That boy of mine is a mess. My husband

died over two decades ago, and I've barely dated since then. Now, I bring a great man around and Damien doesn't know how to act right."

"Mary, I'm sure he's just being protective. He'll come around."

"I sure hope so," she sadly replied.

CHAPTER 30

Chamberlayne (Damien)

The next morning, the sound of a vacuum cleaner woke me up. For a second, I sat up in bed, thinking back to the night before with my mom and her guests. *Was I wrong for being so short with the guy?* I could be a bit overprotective of my mother, and I knew that sometimes I went overboard. What should people expect though? She was all I had. I'd thought I had Janet too, but that was obviously fake. Sitting up in bed, I grabbed my phone and surfed Instagram. Groupies of all shapes and sizes were sending me direct messages full of nude poses. At one time, this kind of stuff turned me on, but now I thought it just showed how these women had no class or self-respect, and that they had an agenda. Who would send a man whom they don't even know, butt naked photos? No woman I would ever seriously date would do something like that. A soft knock came, then the door pushed slightly open.

"What do you have planned today?" my mom

asked.

"Well, I wanted to show Maya around. Then I was going to stop and see Tony so I can get a cut and maybe shoot hoops with some of my boys. Nothing too much, just happy to be home."

"Sounds good. I have breakfast waiting downstairs for you. Maya's already down there. I'm going to clean up this house and maybe do a little sewing."

It was then that I realized there were dark circles surrounding her eyes and bags underneath.

"I wish you would let me get you a maid or something, mom. This place is already clean, I don't know why you bend over backwards to overdo things."

"You worry about you and I worry about me and you," she smirked. Closing the door, I showered and was at the table to eat in less than an hour. Maya looked so comfortable and at home. Fully dressed and ready for the day, I marveled at how beautiful my attorney was. This was weird, but for the first time in forever, I thought someone was beautiful, but didn't have an urge to bed or date her. She was like a long lost cousin or something.

For half the day, we drove around and made several stops. A few times, I noticed a sad look come over Maya's face. It was as if she had left Richmond with bad memories and returning was like opening a closed casket. It wasn't until we went back to the apartment complex on Chamberlayne Avenue that she looked like she had seen a ghost.

The building looked like it did every time I passed by it. The red bricks were weathered and glass was shattered throughout the area. Probably from gunshots or robberies.

"We can leave if you're uncomfortable," I said.

"No, let's look around for a second."

Unsure where we were going exactly, I parked the car in between a Honda Civic and a Mazda, and we walked up the steps, with Maya leading. It was as if she knew exactly where to go. On the second floor, we paused as a junkie flew past us, looking strung out. His scratching himself and speaking out loud, made me feel sad to know that there were people who actually lived like that. Maya stood in front of Apartment 207, and I watched nervously as she knocked on the door. This place was giving me the creeps. Roaches ran past us and trash littered the whole area. It was dirty, to put it kindly, and it made me want to go home and take another shower. I was no stranger to the hood, but this building seemed so recognizable and unsafe. After several moments, a young woman answered.

"Can I help you?" she asked with an attitude.

"Hi, I'm Maya and this is Damien," she began. "I used to live here."

Rolling her eyes, the woman looked us both up and down before turning around. Looking over her shoulder, I noticed her gaze fall on a young boy sitting in front of the TV. Looking back at us, she perched her hand on her hip and finished asking us questions.

"Ohhhhhkay, well welcome back to paradise. Again, how can I help you?" she asked sarcastically. Nervously, Maya played with the ring on her right hand and kept talking.

"Can we come in for a second? This place has a lot of memories and I just want to take a look around."

With a twist of her neck, the woman sucked her teeth and told us to come inside. Moving her body out the doorway, she waved us into the small space.

"It ain't clean, but since you look like you going through something and need closure, come on in."

The apartment was small, and a child who looked around three or four sat quietly in the living room watching Cartoon Network. Maya looked like she was in a trance, as she stayed rooted at the door. Grabbing her by the hand, I led her around the apartment until she was in a puddle of tears. After looking inside the bedrooms, kitchen, and living room, it was time for us to head out.

"Thank you so much for letting us come inside your home," I whispered to the tenant, who later told us her name was Kenya. While I talked to her, Maya looked out of the window that overlooked the development. I discreetly slid the woman $500 as thanks for letting us disrupt her day. I could tell this moment meant a lot to Maya, and I wanted to make sure Kenya knew that as well. With a look of surprise, Kenya suddenly cried as well. *What was it about these women and their crying?*

"I'm sorry," she said while wiping her tears. "My son's birthday is coming up and I didn't know what I was going to do about getting him presents this year. It's hard being a single mother with no help and a piss poor job. Thank you so much."

Making a mental note, I just smiled. It made me happy to do things for others, especially for those who I believed were good people. Kenya seemed like a good person who was just in a messed up situation. A more composed Maya came over to us.

"Thanks for bringing me here, Damien, I'm ready to go when you are."

With those words, we were off. I was going to drop Maya off at the house, stop by the shop, and then meet up with my boys. Before getting out of the car, she turned to me with red puffy eyes, and gave me some advice.

"I think you need to apologize to your mom. She's a beautiful woman and you should be happy that there's a man in her life who appreciates her beauty and kindness. He seems like a nice man, Damien."

Her words echoed in my brain as I pulled up to my old barbershop. She was right and I was being selfish. For a second, I sat behind the wheel and noted the changes that had been made to the outside of the building. Nice to know my money was being used in the right way, I thought to myself. Tony was the owner and he'd been cutting my hair for years. After I blew up, I decided to invest some money into his business, making it one of the best barbershops to visit in the Richmond area. The door clinked open and Tony was right there, clippers in hand ready to cut my hair.

"My man," I said, while dapping up one of the few people I actually considered family. He was older than I was, and like a big brother. The other men in the shop nodded at me and thankfully, no one tried to spark up a basketball conversation or anything else. That was the good thing about coming home; people treated me just like they did before I became a millionaire athlete.

"What's up D! Nice seeing you man."

For the duration of my time there, we caught up on each other's lives. Being the respectful person that he was, Tony didn't mention my legal situation, not once. This was why I loved the dude. He always let me bring things up first. As he cut my hair, I sat still in the seat, reflecting on my recent drama. The clippers stopped, and I couldn't help my next words.

"I didn't do it man."

"I know you didn't, D. I know you."

I released a deep breath as he said those words. It felt good to know people actually had my back.

CHAPTER 31

Dirty Little Secret (Damien)

Hours later, I banged open the front door and was greeted by silence. It was then that I noticed my mom and Maya sitting in the small room near the dining room table with Mrs. Oliver.

"Hey baby," my mom called. "Mrs. Oliver is here. She said she had something important to talk to us about."

At this point, I knew my mother's neighbor was a nut job. What did this stranger have to share with people she didn't even know? Walking into the room, I looked at Maya's face for a sign, but got nothing. She seemed uncomfortable. Sitting down, I dropped my keys on the table and waited for the lady to speak. The older woman, who still looked good for her age, cleared her throat and began.

"Maya, remember when I said you looked familiar? Well, I went home last night and almost instantly remembered. I want to share a story with you all. I have been a registered nurse for a very long time and have seen many people come through my hospital right here in Richmond. Anyway, there was one particular incident that was vastly different from many others. One night many years ago, I received news of a homicide-suicide. In rushed the paramedics with a young boy who happened to be around one-years-old and was having trouble breathing due to multiple seizures. An older woman then came in with a young girl who was around seven or eight. She had the biggest eyes. Kind of reminds me of Tracee Ellis Ross's eyes. She was the little boy's sister. That night the little girl lost both of her parents, and was hoping her brother would live."

A slight gasp escaped Maya, and the look she had worn earlier during our trip to the ghetto was the gaze she had now. The eyes comment made me zero in on hers. Damn, her eyes kind of reminded me of the actress's. I had never asked Maya about her biological parents because I felt it was none of my business. I lost both of my parents and knew how sensitive a topic it was to discuss. Realizing that this story probably involved my lawyer, I concentrated more on Mrs. Oliver's words.

"Not long after arriving, the young boy appeared to be dead. News was given to the elderly woman, whom we later found out was a neighbor. She grabbed the young girl's hand and led her outside of the hospital. Not long after that, the monitor suddenly picked up tiny electrical movements. The young boy seemed to still be alive."

Clutching her heart, Mrs. Oliver took a break, then continued.

"Dr. Raja Nazir gave the word and the team began working on the little boy again. Very slowly, the heart rate picked up. He survived. With no paperwork or information on the next of kin, the team reached out to a caseworker and the young boy was placed into foster care once he was stable. It hurt my heart that he wouldn't at least be with his sister, but there was nothing we could do. We didn't know the name of the young girl or the older woman who had accompanied her."

Maya was in a fit of tears and I wanted to comfort her. Turning to me, Mrs. Oliver posed her next question.

"Damien, how did your parents die?"

"I don't know much about them, but in the file the case workers sent along to my foster mother, it said that my dad killed my mom, then himself," I muttered.

"Did you have anything happen to you as a child?"she continued.

Thinking back, I was irritated about her line of questioning. Wasn't this about Maya?

"Ummm, not that I know of."

"Damien had multiple seizures as a baby," my mom said in a daze. "It was in his medical file when I adopted him."

"You never told me that, ma," I said, irritated. It was then that things began to click.

"Remember the place we visited today? The apartment where I said I used to live?" Maya joined in.

Nodding my response, she continued. "Well, you did too. I'm sorry, Damien, my parents just told me a different version of this story a couple of months ago. I didn't know how to bring it up to you. I had already taken you on as a client."

Realization settled in, and I fought to keep my emotions under control.

"I'm your sister."

Moments went by before I responded.

"I knew I had a sister. I couldn't remember any names and I would ask my different foster families about her, but they always said there was no real information about my family besides that of my parents getting killed. I knew I wasn't crazy."

Jumping to my feet, rage took over, and I grabbed my keys off the table and headed for the front door. Punching a hole next to the window, I ran to my car with everyone following behind.

"Baby, come back. Let's talk about this, you're in no shape to drive."

Ignoring my mom, I revved the engine and was out.

***

Staring at the basketball courts that I used to play on as a child, I cursed quietly under my breath. Guys I had never seen before were playing a game, but I couldn't focus on them. Staring off into space, I began reliving old memories.

Shuffling us in one by one, the handcuffs around my wrists felt like a heavy brick was resting on them. In my thick jumpsuit, I lined up, waiting for my name to be called. "This shit is stupid," I mumbled.

"No talking boy!" yelled one of the correctional officers. I cut my eyes at the overweight thirty-something year-old black man standing just a few feet from me. Ignoring him, I looked down at the floor and waited for my name to be called. After ninety minutes of standing in the hallway behind eight others, I heard someone call my name. Pushing me forward, the Uncle Tom of an Officer almost knocked me over as he guided me through the door.

"Yo man, chill," I snapped. I didn't care where I was or who he was, no one was about to disrespect me. I learned early on that you had to grab respect from people, or they would punk you. Instead of responding, Officer Luke, whose name was listed on his nametag, just grunted. I guess he figured there was no point in lashing out at me, since I would probably be put away anyways. Walking to my seat next to my court appointed lawyer, I took a quick glance around the room and saw only one person I knew, Mrs. Roseland, there to support me. With a slight nod

of acknowledgment, I turned around and took my seat. That day I was charged with a drug possession violation and was sentenced to two years in juvie.

Snapping back to reality, I gritted my teeth, a bad habit I picked up as a kid. Fuck Maya's apology. Everything that I'd been through couldn't be erased. It was unfair that while she was living lavishly, I was living a nightmare. Leaning against the fence, someone nearby called out to me.

"Yo! Damien Roseland, is that you?" an excited boy asked.

"Hey man, how are you?" I responded.

"I'm okay, but they're not letting me ball with them."

Looking at the young teenager, he reminded me a lot of myself at that age. Putting my arms around his shoulders, I led him onto the court.

"You're with me. We're both going to play."

The boys on the court stopped dribbling the ball as we grew closer. Thrilled and happy to have their hometown hero there, they welcomed me, plus my new friend, to a new game. This was the perfect remedy to get my mind off of the mess going on around me.

CHAPTER 32

Timely Departure (Maya)

"Maya, are you sure you don't want to stay and talk to Damien?" Mary asked.

"No, I think he needs his space. We'll talk when he gets back to Washington, but again, thank you for everything, Mary."

Before she could further try and persuade me to stay, I jumped out of the car and grabbed my suitcase from the backseat. Damien had left the house hours ago and never returned. Something told me it would be best to head back home, so I booked a one-way ride on the train. Getting out of the car to give me a hug, Mrs. Roseland grabbed me into a tight embrace.

"We will get through this, honey, just please keep in touch with me.

After promising to call regularly and to continue helping her son with his case, I was finally headed home. I called Taylor to make sure she could pick up me at the train station and then I settled into my seat for the short ride. This trip was the hardest one I'd ever had to take.

Leaning against my window, I watched the trees and scenery go by. Grabbing my phone, I figured it would be best to stay busy instead of thinking of everything that had just happened. After leaving a voicemail for my mother to let her know I was okay, I logged onto Facebook. Social Media wasn't big on my to-do list but when I had time, I always signed on to snoop on old friends and family members. It seemed like my newsfeed was always full of people getting married or having babies. Bored with what I read, I clicked open my personal email account and saw a message that made me sit up straight in my seat.

"Be careful," said the message. "Drop Damien's case. Take this as your second warning."

No name was attached to the message, but I knew people who could trace the email back to the sender. For some reason, the warning gave me chills. Before thinking further, my phone vibrated.

"What you doing baby?" Vince asked when I picked up.

I heard noises in the background and could make out the faint sound of dice being thrown on a table amidst a sea of laughter.

"Headed home, what are you up to?"

I hadn't told Vince of my trip to Richmond, for the sake of privacy, and I know Damien hadn't either.

"You work too hard, Maya," He said, ignoring my question."Let's do something fun tomorrow. I can come by around noon to get you."

Vince's condo wasn't far from mine so it was convenient for us to see one another. The email I'd just received had me a little shaken, but instead of voicing my concerns, I decided to ignore it.

"Really?" I asked. "I'm excited. I'll be ready to see you at noon."

CHAPTER 33

Blast to the Past (Damien)

The game went great, but as soon as it was over, my mind went right back to reality. Walking to my car, I looked straight ahead at the houses that lined the streets. With my hands deep into my pockets, I knew there was one place I needed to visit before heading back home to face my mother and Maya. I decided to go to my old foster home to see Fran, hoping to get some answers. Just as Maya needed closure, I suddenly did too.

"What the hell you doing back around here?" Fran asked as she opened the rickety screen door. She was wearing a housecoat and a beat-up and smelly silk scarf. "I ain't got no room for you. My new man turned your old room into a cigar place for him and his boys so you can't stay here again."

Her smirk pissed me off, but I decided to ignore it until I got the information I needed.

"I just want to find out what you know about my real family. Do you remember anything?"

It had been more than a decade since I last lived with Fran, but I figured she would know something since I was with her for the duration of my childhood. Slowly, her smirk turned into a sinister laugh. She snickered so hard that her body fell against the wall next to the doorway. Trying to control my anger, which was slowly building up, I stood straight up, with a blank stare, waiting on her to answer. It seemed like ten minutes went by before she finally gained control of herself.

Grabbing her hefty stomach, she said, "Well, boy, all I know is what your case worker told me. She just said that your ole drunk daddy went crazy and shot your mama, and almost shot you. That's all I got for you."

Disgusted by her, I turned around and headed for the door. My time there was a waste. Before making it outside, a man weighing at least 400-pounds came out of the bedroom. *This has to be Fran's new man*, I thought. The way he was rubbing his eyes made me think he had been asleep before Fran interrupted him with her loud voice. Looking at me, recognition came to him.

"Damien Roseland? Power Forward for the Washington Cougars now?" Like a kid on Christmas Day, the big burly man rushed up to me and grabbed me into a bear hug. Standing in her spot, Fran pasted on a smile and walked towards us.

"Cougars, now D?" she asked while rubbing my arm. Turning to her man, she said, "You know

I raised him right?"

Seeing where this was going, I threw off my former foster mother's arm and headed out the door without another word. They weren't worth it. Following behind me, Fran began to toss her hands in the air while demanding I give her a cut of my money. Then, out of nowhere she busted out singing the theme song from the Jefferson's, "Movin on up, to the east side."

While walking down the street and back to my car, I still heard her singing. As she danced on her stoop, the last thing I heard was, "We finally got a piece of the pieeee!"

An hour later, I sat in my car in front of my mom's house and just cried. Minutes went by before the front door opened. Quietly, mom opened up the driver's side door and led me in the house. Inside, just as she would do when I was younger, she held me and rocked me back and forth until my tears stopped.

PART III

CHAPTER 34

Breakthrough (Maya)

Lying back in the bed, I thanked God for the millionth time for putting Vince in my life. I still hadn't told him about my connection to Damien, but it felt nice to have him there the next day when I arrived home from my trip to Richmond. The draft from the nearby window made me stand up in all my naked glory and cross the room to close it. Rushing back to the warmth of Vince's sheets, I buried myself underneath and placed my hands behind my head. The shower steadily ran, and movement could be heard from inside the bathroom. Vince took his shower time very seriously and hated to be disturbed. A bright light flashed on my phone and I wondered who could be calling me at this late hour. Detective Townsend's, or Corey as he instructed me to call him, name flashed across my screen, causing me to immediately sit up. I hadn't heard from him since I first gave him my business card months ago. Making sure the water was still running, I pushed Talk on the phone.

"Hello?"

"Hi Maya, it's Corey, is this a good time for you?"

"Well, sure, what's going on? Is Damien ok?"

"For now he is, but I wanted to let you know that there's been a break in the case. A friend of mine who has been working on your case let it slip to me that there is video footage from a camera on a nearby lamppost shows that someone left the area soon after Janet was raped. The car didn't belong to Damien; it belonged to a member of his team. A person with a rather long history of gambling debts."

Before my new friend could finish, the water in the bathroom stopped and my heart seemed to be caught in my throat.

"Are you familiar with a Vincent James, Maya?"

I didn't have time to respond. Vince quietly reentered the room with a towel wrapped around his waist. I discreetly hung up from the call and placed my phone on silent.

"Baby, what are you doing up? You want more, don't you?"

An arrogant smile graced his lips as he wiped the remaining water from his face. His sex game was okay, but not the best I'd ever had. Why did guys always think their ability to make love was the best?

"A client, called me. She's nervous about how

her case will work itself out."

"Well, I hope you told her that she's working with the best in the game and not to worry about anything."

With that, Vince released his towel and slid back into the bed. His hard body rolled on top of me, his piece plummeting inside of my body. Thoughts of the detective's words sank to the back of my head. There was no way that my Vince could be involved in such a heinous crime. Before we finished making love, my eyes grazed the light from my phone. A text had come in. I didn't get a chance to grab it as Vince continued making my body do things I didn't know it could do. For the first time since we started having sex, I wasn't into the lovemaking. All I could think about was what Corey had said, and I wondered if I had been sleeping with the enemy.

CHAPTER 35

No Solution (Maya)

Sorting through my mail, I noticed a pretty beige envelope that had come from Ivey. The contents of the package made me grin, and I couldn't wait to share the exciting news with Taylor. I made a mental note to call my friend later to thank her. Turning my attention to my personal emails, I opened my Gmail account, and sat back in my seat to locate the threatening email I'd received a week earlier. Not only had I received this message, but someone had been calling me nonstop and hanging up. I decided to hand this information over to Corey in hopes of uncovering who was sending me the threatening notes. After forwarding the information, Damien's face popped inside my doorway. My assistant was right behind him.

"I'm sorry, he insisted on seeing you even without an appointment."

Sliding my glasses off my face, I stood up from my seat and motioned for Damien to come inside.

"It's fine, Annette, I wanted to see him anyway."

Damien walked into the office as if he owned the place, leaving Annette in the hallway looking nervous. Nodding in her direction, I smiled to let her know that everything was okay. Once the door was closed, I sat back in my seat and waited to hear the reason for his visit. With one foot crossed over his leg, Damien leaned forward and smacked my desk.

"What's up sis!"

Catching me off guard, I sat up, stunned, in my seat.

"That's what you want to hear, right?" He continued. "You want me to forgive and forget, right? Anyway, I stopped by to tell you that you're fired. Your services are no longer needed; I'm going to go with another person in your firm. I'm sure you know Charles Anderson."

Damien's smirk told me his mind was made up and that there was no use in trying to change it. At a loss for words, I sat with my mouth open before catching myself. I didn't blame him for not wanting to work with me anymore.

"If you would feel more comfortable doing that, then I respect your decision."

Though I knew him dropping me would look bad for my career, I could see where he was coming from. I wasn't fond of Chuck, based on our last encounter. Plus, although he'd been practicing law for a while, he honestly was still one of the worst attorneys at the firm, but it was Damien's choice, not mine.

Standing up, his fake smile turned into a frown as he leaned toward my desk and whispered angrily, "You will never be my damn sister." With that, he turned his back on me and headed towards the door.

"Damien," I began weakly. Ignoring my call, he turned left, in the direction of Chuck's office. Once the door was closed behind him, I collapsed on my desk in defeat. Why did I feel emptier than the day when I thought I'd lost my family? It was only nine in the morning but I knew I had to take a few hours away from the office. Phoning Annette, I instructed her to jot down messages for me until 2:00 p.m. Speeding out to the garage, I called Taylor, who promptly cancelled her morning appointments to meet me at our favorite bagel shop off of New York Avenue.

Placing my car in park, I hopped out the car, barely closing the door behind me. I was emotional and wanted to see a friendly face. Sitting with her legs crossed at a table close to the entrance, Taylor stood to greet me. For several seconds, she gave me the hug that I had been desperately craving. Taking my seat, I noticed she had already ordered my favorite cup of coffee and bagel sandwich. With her hair pulled back into a high bun, Taylor looked more stunning than ever in her designer suit.

"Girl, if I didn't know any better I would think

you had a man or something," I said in a lighthearted voice. My attempt to lighten the mood seemed to work because Taylor beamed at my comment.

"Well," she began. "I have met someone, but I'm taking things slow. That's why I haven't mentioned anything about him to you or Ivey."

The thought of Taylor having a man was enough to make me forget all my problems for the moment. I tried asking a few questions, but she kept dismissing them.

"I'll tell you guys the details when the time is right. I don't want to jinx this thing," she nonchalantly said.

Before I could comment, my phone rang. "Sorry," I mouthed to her as I picked up the unfamiliar caller. As I went to answer, Taye's cell went off as well. A frown crossed her face as she stood up to step outside to take it. Ignoring her, I greeted my caller.

"Hello, Attorney Kincaid here...Hello?"

Before I could hang up, I heard the caller breathe heavily into the phone.

"Please stop playing on my phone," I said.

"Maya, take this as your third official warning."

With that, the call was disconnected.

"This is getting ridiculous," I said out loud. Turning towards the window, I saw Taylor pacing back and forth on the sidewalk. Whoever called her had definitely put her on edge. I hoped it wasn't her new guy. Moments later, she walked back inside, her eyes red. I decided to tell her about the prank calls later. Whoever called her definitely had made her sad and I needed to make sure she was going to be okay.

Taylor Desmond, raised by her paternal grandmother, whom she often referred to as Nana, had lived a hard life. At a young age, her mother tried to put her up for adoption in exchange for drugs, while her father was in and out of jail for various charges. Eventually, Taye's dad caught a twenty-year drug charge, which soon led to her mother's disappearance. Though Nana provided support and love for Taye, growing up in Philadelphia was not easy on her. Constantly surrounded by drugs and crime, it was a miracle that the girl graduated Summa Cum Laude from high school and went off to college. At the age of thirteen, Taye knew it was her job to take care of herself and her Nana. Dreaming of living in a big fancy house and having a stable lifestyle is what encouraged her to go into business and real estate.

"David called me," she started. "He's locked up again and needs my help."

David Desmond was Taylor's biological dad, and a pain in her ass. After serving his twenty-year bid, he had only been out from behind bars for a few months. Obviously, he was back in.

"He told me to call my sisters and to come up with some money to get him out. I hung up on him, then he called back and left me a message.

Another jailbird probably let him use his call time. Hear, listen."

"They think I'm dealing drugs again baby girl, but I ain't! I need your help…" Before he could continue, the automated voice service came on to tell us that the call had been disconnected.

Shaking her head, Taye just sat there holding the phone, with a blank stare in her eyes. The stare soon changed to anger and then quickly back to sadness as she grabbed my shoulder to cry on. As I rubbed her back and held her in my arms, all I could say was, "I'm here for you."

After a few minutes, I decided to take her to the spa down the street. Why can't she ever catch a break? I asked myself. She worked so hard to take care of her family. For a couple of hours, we both received massages, hoping that the temporary relief would have a lasting result. Afterwards, I decided to surprise her further.

"Guess what Ivey sent me?" I said to her as we sat in robes while getting pedicures.

Without waiting for her to respond, I threw the VIP tickets to the concert that I had received by mail earlier and started the chorus to 99 Problems.

"Were going to see Jay-Z and Beyoncé next week!"

Finally flashing her beautiful smile, Taye giggled and said, "Yesssssss! Ohmigod I have to find something to wear!"

"Not only that," I continued. "Ivey was asked to host the Evening with the Stars event this year in Cali and she invited us, along with her mother!"

Taylor's loud squeal carried through the spa. People were looking at us, but we could care less. Things seemed to be looking up.

For the next week, I drowned myself in work. With Damien's case now water under the bridge, I was able to focus more on some of my other clients. It was 6:00 p.m. on Thursday evening when I decided to leave work. As I was locking up, I felt someone walking up behind me. Turning around, my eyes locked with Chuck's. Feeling uncomfortable with how close he stood next to me, I scooted to the side to widen the distance between us.

"Maya, I want to apologize for what happened a few months ago."

Surprised at how sincere he sounded, I let him continue.

"I shouldn't have been so disrespectful to you or my wife. Please accept my apology."

"It's fine Chuck, thank you for bringing this up. I've been feeling very uncomfortable around you since that day."

Nodding his head, I could tell he still felt uneasy around me too.

"Well, as I'm sure you know, I'm helping Damien Roseland now with his case. I was hoping you could assist me with it since you've been working on it."

For several seconds, I debated his offer. Had it not been for Damien I would have probably told him no, but something told me I needed to lend a hand.

"Sure Chuck," I said with finality. "Let's meet up soon and I will share my file on him with you."

With that, I shook his hand and headed out the door. I was running late and the concert started in a couple hours.

CHAPTER 36

Plan of Destruction (Vince)

The trial was set for next month and I was getting nervous. Taking a quick swallow of my whiskey and coke, I glanced up at the beauty who sat across from me at a table by the bar. She calmly sipped on her red wine in the hotel lounge while glancing down occasionally to look at her cell phone. Moments went by before she finally sat her glass down. Staring at me with piercing eyes that had a hint of blue in them, I squirmed under her gaze. She was the boss, and sometimes it made me queasy to know that.

"Well, what do you have for me, Vince?"

In an effort to stay incognito, she pulled down the brim of her hat to cover her eyes even more.

"Well, since we found out a few weeks ago that Maya is Damien's biological sister, I figured having her on the case would complicate things, so I found a different lawyer to handle his case. The calls and texts you've been making to her haven't been working. She's a smart girl and I underestimated her. We should be in the clear now, with the new lawyer, though. He doesn't have the best record, which will work in our favor."

I was still amazed at how much Damien trusted me. Just days after returning from his trip to Richmond, he opened up about finding out that Maya was his blood sister. I almost shit my pants when he told me, but I had to keep it cool. Knowing how passionate Maya was about her clients, I knew it would be best to get her off his case. I had no doubt that she would work even harder for him, knowing that he was her brother. I was still seeing Maya, just because I wanted to keep her close in case something popped off. She didn't know that I knew the truth, and that's how I wanted it to stay.

"We better be fine, Vincent," my companion said in a composed voice. "I like you, a lot, but what I want, I get. Right now I want Damien out of the league."

I didn't understand why she was going through all this to get rid of Damien, but I knew better than to ask questions. My assessment was that she was still bitter about him dumping her.

"Now business is over, I'll see you again soon."

Standing up from my stool, I followed the beauty through the lobby, and to the parking lot. Her switch alone made me salivate. She looked so good but her bossiness and aggressiveness always threw me off. She wasn't my type.

CHAPTER 37

99 Problems, but Your Opinion Ain't One (Damien)

The clock struck 7:55 p.m. just as I pulled into the busy Verizon Center parking lot. Next to me, my date clapped with excitement as I turned the car off and slid the key out of the ignition.

"This is going to be great," she beamed.

Getting out of the driver's seat and running around to open her door, I couldn't help but roll my eyes at her. Tasha Edwards was definitely a beauty. With full lips, wide eyes, and a body to kill, she caught the attention of every guy who walked by. Though I was immediately attracted to her, my attraction began to fade as soon as she opened her mouth. The girl was both ditzy and vain, two things Janet was far from being. In fact, it was her fault that we arrived to the concert late.

"Come on Tasha, we have to hurry … the concert starts in a few and we still have to get backstage."

As she rolled her body out of the car, I was reminded of why I put up with her bland personality. The girl looked good!

Quickly grabbing her hand and shutting her door, we swiftly walked to the entrance of the exclusive section of the arena and flashed our tickets. As we walked through the large center, I dapped up a few basketball fans. In just a few short months of playing for the Cougars, it seemed like everybody embraced and loved me. Backstage, I was able to see celebrities from everywhere. I was happy to know that Tasha wasn't star struck because the amount of pop stars, rap legends, and actors in attendance was enough to make anyone excited, even me, on the low. I was able to dap up a lot of major performers before they went on stage. Soon after, we left to take our seats in the VIP section.

As soon as we reached our spots, the lights began to dim and the first act came onstage. I could barely pay attention to the local group as Tasha's hand began to travel down the middle of my jeans. I enjoyed the sensation I felt from her small, yet firm hand.

"We're going to have a good night," Tasha whispered in my ear. I smiled back knowingly. It had been a while since I'd hung out on a date. I had taken Maya's advice seriously when she was my lawyer, and stayed away from the scene; but now that she wasn't my attorney, I kicked her and all her advice to the curb.

As the local acts left the stage, I heard a cough behind me. Turning to my right, I noticed a familiar pair of eyes, even in the dark. It was

Maya, my dear sister. Sending her a head nod, I never received anything in return. Instead, she pointed to Tasha's hidden hand, which had somehow disappeared into my jeans. With a look of disappointment, Maya turned her attention back to the stage.

Fuck her, I thought to myself. That girl is way too uptight and she's no longer my lawyer so her opinion doesn't matter. Before I could fully let her attitude get to me, I felt the people in the stands go crazy as the beat to 99 Problems came on. It was finally show time, and nothing else mattered. Ignoring the vibration coming from an incoming phone call, I pushed Tasha's hand off of me and jumped to my feet. I rocked to the beat as Jay made his way to the stage.

"Now this is living," I mumbled.

***

"You know you can come inside, right?" Tasha eagerly said as she guided me towards her front door.

As much as I wanted to follow her into the house, I knew it would be against my better judgment. Sex would likely end our night if I walked through that door. Fear stopped me from pursuing it. I couldn't put myself in another bad situation, especially with this case looming over me.

"Naw T, I had a good time with you tonight, though. I have practice in the morning." In reality, I was ready to get rid of this freak. She was too much, and I had an inkling that she was nothing more than a gold digger. With a hug, I left a scowling Tasha on the steps and headed back to my Range Rover. Once settled in the cushioned leather seats, I felt my phone vibrate, with MOM flashing across the screen.

With a sigh, I picked up.

"Whose parents are up at two a.m. on a weekday, Ma?" I asked with a smile.

"One who's concerned, where've you been? I've been worried."

"Yea Ma, I'm good, just left a concert not too long ago. Why do you keep calling? I told you I'm fine."

"Well, after all that's been happening, can you blame me?" she asked with sadness in her voice.

"I'm okay Mom, I promise. Now go to sleep."

"Okay baby. I love you."

"Love you more, ma."

CHAPTER 38

Premiere Day (Ivey)

"Your face is beat, Ms. V!"

Since I'd arrived in the land of the famous and fun, everyone around me had begun to call me V, and I was really starting to take a liking to it.

"Thanks, Brandon," I beamed at him before facing the mirror in front of me. It was the night of the movie premiere and I was a bundle of nerves.

Within minutes of finishing my hair and make-up, a swarm of stylists surrounded me with various articles of clothing in their hands, ranging from Valentino, Gucci, and Piucci to Jimmy Choo, Christian Louboutin, and Giuseppe. It looked like one person specialized in the jewelry, another took care of the shoes, and one the clothes. Everything happening around me seemed unbelievable! After fitting into my custom-made Stella McCartney dress, my assistant ran to me with my business phone in her hands. "Ms. Walden, your friend Maya is on the phone for you, she wants to know..."

Before she could finish her sentence I snatched the iPhone from her hand and turned the speaker feature on, refusing to mess up my makeup after spending hours in that chair.

"Hey, girl! What's up? Where y'all at? Is my mom with you?"

"Dang, can I answer one question at a time?" Maya laughed. "Me, Taye, and your mom are in the limo heading to the show now! We're so excited!"

Ignoring the hustle and bustle going around me, I walked out of my dressing room so that I could make sure I heard everything Maya had to say.

"Can't wait to see you guys! I've missed you!"

"Well that's about to change in a few. We'll call you when we get to the carpet."

Hanging up from our talk, I leaned against the wall. Wow, this is really happening. Before I could think and reminisce any further, a tall figure came around the corner. With a smile on his lips, I knew it was definitely show time. Grabbing me in a passionate hug, Ian nuzzled his face in my hair.

"It's going to be great, baby," he whispered. Lost in his arms, I just moaned my response. Then he said, "Daddy has something for you, too."

Squealing like a teenager, I lifted my head and greeted my boyfriend with a kiss of gratitude. Heading in the opposite direction of my dressing room, we moved quickly down the hallway to his suite. After our session, I strategically dusted the white powder from around my nose and smiled brightly. This would be a night to remember.

CHAPTER 39

Lights, Camera, Action! (Maya)

Leather seats, expensive champagne, and good music are the best ways to describe our ride to Ivey's premiere. Feeling large and in charge, I spread myself over the seat cushions and reveled in the feeling. So this was how it felt to be a superstar's best friend? I could get used to this. I was feeling like Rihanna's best friend, Melissa Forde. Chuckling to myself, I gazed out the window to take in the L.A. scene.

"It's gorgeous out here, isn't it?" Ivey's mother asked from the opposite side of the limo.

"Yes, ma'am! We've only been here for an hour and already I'm in love."

"Yeah," Taye chimed in. "This place is like magic."

"Well girls," Ms. Walden continued, "I think it's beautiful too, but I can't put my finger on it. Something doesn't seem right. Has Ivey talked to you guys about her time out here? Aside from her show?"

Looking at each other, Taye and I shook our

heads at the same time.

"Actually, we don't talk a lot anymore," Taye admitted. "We've all been busy these days. I only talk to my girls maybe once every two weeks. And even then, it's briefly."

Letting the words sink in, I realized she was right. At one time, we all talked a million times a day, now we had to schedule appointments for a phone call with one another. Mama Walden must have taken my silence as confirmation. After knowing her for so long, she knew my feelings a lot of times even before I expressed them.

"This new boyfriend of Ivey's ... I just don't trust him. I flew out here a month ago and didn't get a good vibe from him. Please watch out for my baby, girls. She's all I have, and I don't want her getting so wrapped up in the Hollywood life that she forgets who she is."

Taylor and I took a second to digest the words Mama Walden said. Though she used to always be in the streets and was involved in lots of illegal activity, Ivey's mom had since turned her life around, and I believed in her intuition. She was great at reading people, which was another thing I'd learned about her.

"Ladies," the driver announced from the intercom. "We have arrived at the red carpet."

Gasping, our conversation was long gone as we all hurried to make sure we looked good for the cameras. I grabbed my purse, removed my compact, and began to touch up my make-up.

Looking out the window, I became nervous. I practiced my smile and waited for the chauffeur to introduce us to the world. One-by-one, we shuffled out of the car, with Mama Walden leading the pack. With the barrage of questions coming from all directions, our group moved forward until a reporter stepped forward for an interview. Per Ivey's instructions, we were all to meet her there, where she would be speaking with Shawn Johnson of *Entertainment Daily News.*

Unlike the other reporters, Shawn Johnson politely shook all of our hands before proceeding with his questions to Ivey.

Once we made it inside, Ivey headed backstage, while we took our seats and waited for the show to start. Before getting totally settled in my chair, my phone vibrated. Sending Corey's call to voicemail, I then received a text from him.

Maya, this is important and about the case. Please call me as soon as you are alone.

This couldn't be good. Lost in my thoughts, I tried pushing the bad thoughts to the back of my mind. Right then, I needed to focus on Ivey, besides I wasn't Damien's attorney anymore.

Two hours later, we exited the arena. Ivey had done excellent! Her personality was infectious on the stage. Finally, it was time for the after party, where we would meet her new boyfriend. Stepping into the well-decorated venue, we were surrounded by nothing but beautiful people. Ivey joined us once we were inside, holding hands with the man whom I assumed had captured her heart.

"Ian, please meet my two best-friends Taylor and Maya, you've already met my mother."

Ian sure was a looker with his dark-brown complexion and medium build. He could have easily passed for Blair Underwood, honestly. As we spoke further, I began to like him more. He seemed well mannered and very charming. For some reason, Ms. Walden didn't seem too impressed. Ivey made several attempts to engage her mother in conversation, but instead, she stood to the side and watched Ian like a hawk. This was so unlike her, as she was usually as bubbly and lively as her daughter. Finally, after handing me her clutch bag, Ivey took her mother by the elbow and led her away. I figured she wanted to lighten the mood and introduce her to other partygoers. With the three of us left behind, we chatted briefly before Taye and I excused ourselves to the bathroom. After a quick touch-up in the mirror, we headed back out to the party. On the way out, someone accidentally bumped into me, causing me to drop my purse, as well as Ivey's, which I was still holding for her. The contents of both small purses flew out and fell on the floor. Quickly bending down, Taylor helped me put the items back inside the bags. A sharp breath stopped me from collecting everything when I noticed the little baggie in Taylor's right hand. She hurriedly buried the item back into Ivey's bag and we headed back into the bathroom. We crouched over a toilet as Taylor opened the bag to find out just what was inside. To our fear, it was what we both thought it was. Cocaine. Our best friend was taking cocaine and we were speechless and scared.

The ride back to Ivey's home was tense. The only one talking was Ivey, who seemed to be oblivious to the silence around her. Ivey hadn't been in L.A. long, so Taye and I hoped we'd come in time to help our friend get rid of her new habit. We didn't speak in the car, out of respect for Mama Walden, who was already concerned. We resolved to speak with Ivey the following morning, once Mama Walden was out of the house and at her spa appointment.

Heading to bed was difficult. This trip was supposed to be joyous, but instead, it turned out to be heartbreaking. I showered and lathered up with my favorite shower gel and retreated to my guest room. Ivey had a nice house in North Hollywood with three bedrooms. Since she insisted on having her mother sleep with her, she was such a mama's girl, Taye and I had our own rooms. Sliding under the covers, my phone rang. It was the private investigator again. I had completely forgotten about him, with everything else happening in California.

"Hey, Corey. I'm so sorry I meant to call you back."

Ignoring my excuse, he talked over me.

"Maya, I was able to have someone trace the calls and emails that you have been receiving. Do you know a Shannon Drayson?"

My heart thumped, this couldn't be good. For some reason the name sounded familiar but I couldn't place it. Grabbing my MacBook from the side of the bed, I powered it on.

"I think I might," I said while logging on.

"Well, she's Jimmy Drayson's daughter. Jimmy is the owner of the New York Knights organization."

As he spoke, I typed the name into the Google search engine and gasped as Shannon's image popped up. It was the girl who interrupted my first dinner with Vince at the restaurant. But why was she threatening me?

"There's more Maya. We were able to find out that Vince owes Shannon more than two million dollars. I'm still trying to connect the dots, but I am thinking this debt has to do with Janet's allegations against Damien. Remember, we still have that security footage of him leaving Janet's house after hours."

This was just too much for me to digest. Tossing my laptop to the side, I lay on my pillow, unsure of what to say.

"Maya, I'm going to let you go for now, but please be careful around Vince. I need you to remain calm around him and act normal, but if you notice anything weird call me immediately."

I nodded, as if he could see me, then turned

the phone off. Tossing the blanket over my body, I endured the worst sleep of my life that night.

CHAPTER 40

Breakfast, Talk and Ivey (Maya)

Pots and pans clanked downstairs, waking me up from my nightmare. Only then did I realize it was reality. Moving out of bed, I knew I needed to face the day. Hopping in the shower, I practiced what I would say to Ivey this morning. Thoughts of my friend, Tinsley's, problems with drugs made me want to cry, knowing that another close friend of mine could get wrapped up into that world. The hot water drowned the salty tears that were steadily falling down my face. I washed up and toweled off. Voices were coming from downstairs so I knew I had to get myself together. Inching down the stairs, I heard a deep voice coming from the kitchen.

"Ms. Walden, this breakfast is amazing. Now I see where Ivey gets her great cooking skills from."

I turned into the kitchen right in time to see the tight smile that Mama Walden gave to Ian.

"Good morning all," I said in a voice that I hoped sounded cheerful. Taylor seemed happy to see me. Everyone in the kitchen seemed uncomfortable, but my presence appeared to loosen the tension just a little. Taking a seat next to Taylor, across from Ian and Ivey, I looked everywhere but at Ivey's face.

"Ok, guys, I need to head out to the spa appointment that Ivey set up for me. A car is outside waiting." Mama Walden said.

Tossing her Louis Vuitton purse over her shoulder, she was clearly in a hurry to exit stage left. I don't think it was the amazing spa day that made her move so fast, either. I'm pretty sure it was the company around her. In a quick dash, she was out the door in five seconds, tops. Turning my attention to the dishes of food in front of me, everyone else did the same.

"So, Ian," Taye said. "What do you have planned for today?"

I could tell my girl was trying to get a feel for whether he would be with us for the remainder of the Saturday. Taking a sip of his coffee, he dabbed the corners of his mouth before answering.

"Hanging with some of my boys who are in town, actually. I was supposed to go golfing with them this morning, but I decided to get to know you ladies more. Ivey talks about you both all the time."

Beaming like she'd won a Grammy, Ivey stared at Ian, with love bursting out of her pupils.

For the next few minutes, we all made small talk. Taye and I tried our best to remain normal. We even cracked a few jokes here and there. Finally, it was time for Ian to leave so he could meet up with his friends. As Ivey walked him out, Taye and I took the time to clear the table and clean up the kitchen. In soft whispers, we decided it would be best to have this discussion with Ivey before going out and having fun for the day.

Once she was back in the kitchen, Taye put on a pot of tea and suggested we sit outside on the patio to catch up. Work was going great for all of us and it seemed that our relationships were too. I decided not to tell the girls about the break in Damien's case until more facts were presented to me. For the first time in a long time, my girlfriends seemed at peace. Before receiving the news last night about Vince, one could say I was, too. Catching Taye's eye, I knew it was now or never. Turning to Ivey, I grabbed her hands and held them for a minute, demanding her to give me eye contact. Instead of beating around the bush, I came out straight to her.

"We're so proud of everything you've been accomplishing, but we also can't help but be worried about you too."

Snatching her hands back, Ivey eyed me before asking what I was talking about.

"This is what she's talking about," Taye said holding up the plastic bag of cocaine.

Grabbing it out of her hands, Ivey turned

angry.

"Where the hell did you get that?"

"That's beside the point. Just know that we know that these are your drugs. What's going on Ivey?"

Still fuming, she stood to leave while denying that they belonged to her.

"Ivey, we're your best friends. We won't judge you, but please be honest with us."

We fought for an hour. Tears flowed, Ivey denied, and Taylor punched a hole in the wall. We all had had bad experiences with drugs. Ivey and Taylor had parents who were drug addicts, while I had an alcoholic father who ended up killing my mother, then himself after a drunken rage. Not only that, but my first best friend, Tinsley, was a recovering drug addict. We'd all taken a front row seat to that lifestyle and knew it wasn't pretty. With a bloody fist, Taylor quietly cried in her hands. It was then that Ivey began to realize the depths of her decisions.

"Ian told me it would help me when I'm on T.V. Everyone out here does it, I didn't think it was a big deal."

"It is a big deal. You're talented and successful without this mess; please don't go down the wrong road. We won't let you. And if Ian put you onto this shit, he needs to go, too."

Eyes wide, Ivey jumped up to defend her man. Pushing her back into her seat, I got right up into her face.

"Remember the day that you came to my house, crying because you walked in on your mother being tricked out by a man for drugs? Ivey, you cried for months. You were so hurt and disgusted. What's different about this situation? A man who gets you on drugs does not love you. And for your information, your mom can tell that something is off. She told us so on the way to the show."

The three of us were quiet for a long time after that.

"I'll get help," Ivey muffled.

For the rest of the morning we flushed all the drugs that she had hidden around the house. Taylor agreed to stay with Ivey for a few weeks while I headed back to the east coast. It would be nice for Ivey to have a good and true friend by her side for a while. What really surprised me was that she agreed to talk to Tinsley, who was currently in town. Though they didn't originally get along, now they had a common battle. I was happy that they would be able to hold each other up and accountable. Now that this issue was resolved, I still had one more to face.

CHAPTER 41

Baggage Claim (Maya)

I swung my bag over my shoulder and prepared to exit the airplane. I hated planes and airports. They were overcrowded with crying babies and slow adults, and after traveling from Cali back to the East Coast I was understandably annoyed, even in first class. Walking off the aircraft behind the big man in front of me, I prayed that Vince was outside so I wouldn't have to wait. I only had two carry-on bags so I didn't need to waste time at baggage claim. The chilly air made me gasp. Cali had been in the mid-70s when I left so I wasn't prepared for this 45-degree wind.

Right in front of me sat a Lambo with all the dressings. I knew it had to be Vince and his new toy that he told me he'd bought. As angry as I was with him, I decided to take Corey's advice and play it cool. Walking up to the passenger door, Vince jumped out on his side to assist me with my bags. At least he was a polite criminal. Standing on my tippy toes in my knee-length boots, I reached up and gave him a kiss on the lips. With him opening my door, I slid onto the heated leather seats and leaned back. Once he was settled on his side, we were off.

"I've missed you," he said.

Touching his thigh, I realized that I'd missed him even more. Why did it seem like every man who entered my life, eventually left?

With the last couple of sleepless nights I'd had at Ivey's, I fell asleep not even five minutes into the drive. I was emotional and exhausted. Mama, my biological mother, always did call me a car baby.

Packing up my Barbie dolls, I stuffed all my toys into the pink bag that mama gave me for Christmas the year before. I watched as she ran around the apartment collecting various items. My baby brother screamed and cried but mama ignored him; instead, she stayed focused on getting things together.

"Where we going mama?"

Stopping in her tracks for a brief second, she looked at me with the wide eyes we both shared and then looked away.

"We're moving to D.C."

I'd never heard of D.C., but figured it must be a fun place judging by how fast mama was packing and trying to get there.

"Well, what about daddy?" I asked.

Looking back at me, a tear slid down her face before she turned away again to continue packing. *She never did answer my question, and I never did ask it again. Once everything was packed in the car, mama settled Junior and me inside before driving through the night. Within the first ten minutes, I was half-asleep. The last thing I remembered hearing was mama say, "I love you, my car baby."*

I don't know if it was all the cussing that woke me up, or my dream, but I sat up in my seat as if a bolt of lightning had struck. Glancing to my left, I noticed Vince was on the phone. Catching my look, he quickly said goodbye to his caller, promising to hit them back later.

"Is everything okay?" I asked.

He nodded yes, but I could tell something was wrong. As soon we pulled into his driveway, I felt relived. Though I wished he'd taken me home, I was just happy to have a bed to lie on soon. For the first time, Vince didn't seem eager to have sex. Something was clearly on his mind. Playing it cool, I ignored him while he left me to take a call. I knew something was up. In the midst of brushing my teeth, I left the electronic toothbrush on as I inched near his study. The door was cracked, which was perfect. I was able to see him and hear everything clearly.

"Just calm down, I just need to keep her close. She doesn't know what I do and it needs to stay like that."

The voice on the other end was audibly upset. With his hand rested on his hip and the other supporting the phone, Vince's knitted brows showed distress.

"Look, I'll get Damien out and settle my debt. We'll still meet tomorrow at the restaurant in the Doubletree so I can update you on everything. Just hang in there a little longer Shannon..."

At the mention of Shannon Drayson's name, my shoulder accidentally hit the door, causing it to fly open. Vince looked up, alarmed. Without so much as a goodbye, he hung up on Shannon. Bracing myself for the worst, I stood up straight and tried to play off my snooping.

"Everything okay baby? Why aren't you in bed?"

My acting skills must have paid off, because just as quickly as he wanted to kill me for interrupting his conversation, he pasted a smile on his face and followed me into the bedroom. The next day I planned to be at that hotel.

CHAPTER 42

I Spy (Maya)

It didn't take long for me to figure out which Doubletree hotel Damien and his friend would be visiting since there were only two of them in town. After a couple of calls, I was able to convince the agent at the front desk of the Arlington location to let me know if Vince had reserved a room. The answer was yes. Hours later, wearing a disguise, I sat with Corey in the lobby. Not only did I rock a long auburn wig, but I also wore glasses and heavy makeup, while my new partner wore a fake mustache and all black clothing. Though Vince had never seen the detective, we had to take extra precautions just in case he did recognize him.

An hour later, Vince waltzed inside with Shannon, who donned a wide brim hat and dark sunglasses. Taking her by the hand, he guided her into the restaurant. Once they were seated at a table near the bar, Corey and I stood and walked towards their area. Once we sat down comfortably on our barstools, just inches away from their booth, we ordered some drinks and waited to hear their conversation. As Vince relayed the most up-to-date information on Damien's case, his guest seemed impressed.

"Well, things went better than we could have ever planned," Shannon's voice said behind us.

"Told you it would work out. He's not going to win this and then we'll be in the clear."

I opened my compact and placed the mirror down in front of me, positioned in a way that allowed me to see their expressions. Both looked at ease and familiar with each other. Their voices suddenly dropped, causing Corey and me to lean back in our seats to catch their next words.

"If you hadn't slept with Damien, I wouldn't be going through this in the first place," Vince muttered angrily.

"Oh, don't blame this on me. No one told you to bet money that you didn't have on that game. This is your fault, not mine. Your jealousy for Damien is what landed you here."

"Maya, are you okay?" whispered a concerned Corey. Nodding his way, a slight shudder took over me.

Although I had been able to research Shannon Drayson, Corey was able to give me more information about the beautiful woman, who happened to be the only child of long-time team owner Jimmy Drayson. The information he shared, stunned me. Apparently, Shannon had been betting against her family's team for years.

Her habits ceased when she became intimately involved with Damien a couple years earlier. After he dismissed her for the older actress, Janet, Shannon made it her mission to teach Damien a lesson. Not only would she take Janet from him, but she also planned to take away the sport that he loved so much. Growing up spoiled, she didn't take the word, "no" kindly, and resented the day that Damien cut things off with her. After a gambling debt from Vince went unpaid, Janet decided to forgive the debt as long as Vince could find a way to get Damien out of the league.

As the perfect ally, Vince despised Damien. Jealous of the life he felt he was supposed to live before his injury, Vince wanted his cocky client to fail. After an intense conversation, he and Shannon devised a plan to get Damien out of the league. Not only would this allow Vince to get out of his financial obligation, it would give Shannon her sweet revenge.

"I still feel bad for the guy though," Vince admitted. "He's been through a lot these last few months."

"Well, that's not our problem, is it?" Shannon snapped harshly.

For the first time since they sat down, I noticed Vince eyeing Shannon with distaste. It was as if he regretted working with her. I watched as the scorned woman took a final sip of her drink and stood up. Following her lead, Vince left cash on the table and followed her to the main lobby where they exited the hotel and went their separate ways. Once they were gone, Corey and I looked at one another in disbelief. We'd cracked the case, and I needed to get home to call Chuck and update him. After insisting I walk to my car alone, I went in the opposite direction of the parking lot as Corey.

"Make sure you call me as soon as you get home," he called out to me.

Nodding in appreciation, I disarmed the car alarm before I noticed that the doors were already unlocked. Brushing off an uneasy feeling, I slid into the driver's seat and fixed the radio station to 95.5. Once I arrived at the stop sign leading to the interstate, my heart jumped in my throat when a hand reached across my shoulder and took control of the steering wheel.

"Put this bitch in park and get in the passenger seat," the person behind me said calmly. A quick glance in the rearview mirror exposed Shannon Drayson's face.

Following her instructions, I parked the car and allowed her to take over.

"Didn't think I would notice you, did you? Thought you were smooth and sneaky didn't you?"

Before I could respond, she continued.

"Just like that damn brother of yours. I got something for your ass."

For the first time, I noticed the metal bat that lay in the backseat of the car. Before I could think further, I felt the hardness of the weapon against the side of my head. The next thing I saw was darkness.

CHAPTER 43

The Rescue (Damien)

Grabbing a towel, I hit the showers and prepared to leave the gym. It was an off day, but I believed in working out daily. Glancing at my phone, I noticed I'd received four missed calls from a number I didn't recognize. No voicemail had been left, but something told me to call the number back.

"Hello, this is Damien, did someone place a call to me earlier?"

"Yes, Damien, I'm Corey Townsend, I'm a private investigator. You don't know me, but I have details pertaining to your case."

Immediately, I tensed up. Who was this cat and why was he calling my phone?

"I know this call seems sudden, but I just wanted to know if you've heard from Maya. She was supposed to give me a call yesterday evening and I haven't been able to reach her."

"Umm, I'm not sure how you got my number, but Maya is no longer representing me. I don't know where she is, and honestly I could care less."

After a brief pause, the stranger cleared his throat and continued.

"Well, she did mention that she was no longer your lawyer; however, please know that she's still been working hard on your case. In fact, we went undercover yesterday and found important information to use for your trial. She was supposed to call Charles Anderson with this information but he says he hasn't spoken with her either."

Damien didn't respond, allowing Corey to continue.

"Damien, she told me about your relationship. I know this is a lot to ask, but I need you. Maya may be in danger. Does the name, Shannon Drayson, sound familiar?"

At the mention of the crazy woman I dated prior to Janet, I almost slammed into the back of the car that was in front of me on the highway. Shannon was actually worse than crazy; she was deranged. Our relationship had taken a fatal attraction approach. The last thing she said to me when I officially broke things off with her was, "You will pay for this."

I'd assumed that I was getting dropped from the team because of that threat. Though I was scared to ask for more details, I prompted the investigator to continue.

"We were in the same area as Shannon last night when she met with Vincent James, and we could tell that the two of them are behind the rape allegations. That's all I can tell you at this point. Your trial is scheduled for a week from now and I'm worried that Maya is in some kind of trouble."

Although I wasn't happy with Maya at this point, I knew what Shannon was capable of. I still believed she was the reason behind me being dropped from the Knights organization. Surprised to hear my agent's name in the same sentence with hers, I was becoming more confused by the minute.

"Shannon just bought a new place out here. I think I need to drive by her house. I just hope it's not too late."

After giving Corey the address, I finally hung up from the call, drove to the next light, and made a U-Turn. If I didn't get to Maya in time, things would go from bad to worse.

CHAPTER 44

Revenge (Maya)

The tightness of the rope binding my hands together woke me up. My fingers had fallen asleep and I felt like a ragdoll. Opening my eyes was a difficult task, as the right one barely cracked open due to the blood and puss crusted over it and sealing it shut. I eventually focused on the cold gray area before realizing that I was tied up in someone's basement. Trying to gather my thoughts, I reflected on the night before. The last thing I remembered was being with Corey in the hotel bar.

A sound came from the door at the top of the stairs in front of me. As soon as the face came through the doorway, my memory rushed back to me. I had been kidnapped and beaten by the woman who was trying to sabotage my brother's life.

I wanted to scream, but the duct tape covering my mouth prevented me from doing so. I was confused about what was going on. Prancing down the stairs towards me, Shannon stopped just feet away from me to dust imaginary lint off her checkered cardigan and to sweep loose strands of hair into her high bun. Standing before me, she presented a look that made me fear for my life.

"I see you're finally awake," she said in a syrupy voice.

Upset at my lack of a response, she snatched the tape off of my lips. When I yelled out in pain, she slapped me hard against my left cheek.

"You're smart, Maya, but I'm a little smarter than you, girl. You're just like that brother of yours. You think you know it all."

Tears wanted to come down my cheeks, but I stopped them before they could start. I couldn't show her that I was down; instead, I needed to be strategic.

"You don't have to do this, Shannon," I whispered.

A retched sound came from the back of her throat before a glob of phlegm landed on the front of my blouse. She'd spit on me before erupting into a fit of laughter. I suppressed the vomit that I wanted to spit out at her, and feeling in control, I offered up one more comment.

"I don't deserve this."

Before she could respond, the doorbell rang, startling Shannon out of her trance. Grabbing the roll of tape, she slapped a new piece on me. Once it was secure, she bounded back up the steps to see who was waiting. Fighting with the ropes tied to my wrists, I knew I didn't have long to try and escape.

CHAPTER 45

Do or Die (Damien)

Leaning against the door, I waited for Shannon to answer. I wasn't sure if she was home since no cars were in her driveway, but she could have parked in the garage. Several minutes went by before I finally heard some movement in the house. A rage came over me as the woman whom I once cared for deeply opened up with a smug look. Shannon was a gorgeous girl, but her heart was ice cold. Months after breaking things off with her, I wondered what I had seen in her in the first place. Finally, I realized that it was probably because she had her own money and came from a powerful family. No matter how much I tried to love her in the way she loved me, I just couldn't. Following our separation, many bad things happened that I couldn't trace back to Shannon, but knew they happened because of her. My tires had been slashed, a brick was thrown through my window in New York, plus Janet swore she saw Shannon in different places. It was as if Shannon was stalking her. I'd also received numerous prank calls that the cops couldn't track. For the first time in over a year, I faced the woman who I knew was capable of all the unexplained acts.

A broad smile graced her face as she looked me up and down.

"Well, isn't this a surprise," she said.

"Cut the crap, Shannon, what's going on?"

Pushing past her, I stood in her living room, looking around. Something definitely wasn't right. Turning back around to face her, I saw a .45 caliber handgun pointed directly at me. Eyes that I once thought were soft and kind, were now red and crazy looking. My breath was caught in my throat as I began to realize the extremity of the situation.

"So this is what it took to get you back to me," Shannon said, with fire in her words.

"All this time I would send you gifts and letters, hoping you'd come back, but having Vince rape Janet, then taking your precious sister, is what finally made you notice me again, hunh?"

Stunned to hear what my scorned ex just told me, I struggled to keep my face expressionless.

"Where is Maya?"

"She's dead, Damien. I killed her. She didn't deserve to live, just like you don't."

I watched Shannon cock the gun and move it so that it was positioned in the center of my forehead. The word, dead, rang throughout my head. My sister was dead and it was all my fault.

Choking back the fear that was threatening to show, I knew that my life was now on the line. Thinking fast, the words that flowed out of my mouth were ones of desperation.

"I never stopped loving you!"

The look on her face told me she didn't believe a word I said. Looking over her shoulder, I noticed a figure sneak inside the house and stand behind Shannon, ready to strike. Seeing this figure gave me the motivation to continue.

"I'm serious, the only reason I ended things is because I didn't think I was good enough for you. Your father always made it seem like he didn't want me around, and it was a lot of pressure. Here I am, the league's bad boy, and I was dating the daughter of one of the most respected owners in the league. There was a lot of pressure."

Lowering her gun, Shannon walked up to me and stared at me with the same crazy look she'd worn earlier. Reaching up to my cheek, she began to rub her palms against my temple. Standing on her tippy toes, she reached up to give me a kiss. I shuddered as I felt her cold lips against mine. With her eyes shut, I figured I'd gotten the best of her. Her eyelids fluttered like she was in the middle of a dream, but they soon flew open when a nearby door burst open with Maya standing on the other side. With a swift move, Shannon turned the gun toward Maya and shot in her direction. Luckily, Corey, the figure who Damien first noticed, had snuck through a back window and was able to stop the gunshot from hitting Maya. Instead, the bullet hit and shattered a nearby vase. Corey threw Shannon on the ground and restrained her. A crying Maya looked on with cuts and bruises dotting her sore body.

Rushing over, and relieved that she was alive, the tears that I'd held back were finally released. Hugging her gently, careful not to hurt her sores, I thanked God for keeping her alive.

"I'm sorry, this is all my fault."

For a moment, I had a flashback of Maya holding on to me as child. Tightening my embrace, I realized that despite our different upbringings my sister had never stopped loving me. Like déjà vu, we sat on the steps leading upstairs and rocked each other back and forth before the police arrived.

CHAPTER 46

The Trial (Maya)

"Mr. Vincent James, where were you the day that Ms. Janet Springer was raped?"

With a hand resting subtly on my hip, I posed the question in a way that prayerfully appeared non-judgmental.

"I was running errands for most of the day, but once I received a call from Damien about a Hollywood party that he wanted me to attend with him, I dropped everything and decided to accompany him for the night."

The courtroom was quiet as I paced in front of the witness stand, gathering my thoughts.

"What type of errands were you running that day?"

Caught off guard by my question, Vince quickly sat up and rattled off a list of activities he had done that day.

"I mean, I ran to the cleaners, car wash, and then the bank. Nothing extreme just some regular weekend chores."

Summing up my ammunition, I stood before the witness stand and gazed at Vincent as if I had all day. "And that's, all you did?"

Jokingly, Vince replied, "I mean I'm sure I used the bathroom or answered a few phone calls in between."

While some of the jury and courtroom members laughed at his response, I didn't find a damn thing funny. In fact, I was getting everything I needed for my ammo. After my kidnapping and reunion with Damien, he saw fit to retain me once again as his attorney. I happily obliged, as I wanted, more than anything, to put these clowns behind bars for a very long time.

"I thought you would say something like that." Looking down at my black suit and Louboutin heels, I looked back up at Vince and noticed a glimmer of fire in his eyes. Looking straight back at the fire, I was determined to continue.

"Was one of the people who you spoke with the daughter of a well-known team owner? You know, Shannon Drayson, the person you owed two million dollars to in a gambling debt?"

Silence followed my question.

"Well, was it?" I asked, unfazed by his discomfort.

"Maybe, but what does that have to do with why we're here?"

Looking over my shoulder to the defendant's table, Damien sat motionless as he listened to his attorney and agent battle.

"It has everything to do with why you're here. Would I be wrong in saying that you and Ms. Drayson had an agreement to get Damien put out of the league so that you would not have to pay her back that hefty sum of money? What better way to frame my client, Mr. Roseland, than for rape; something he didn't do."

"I don't know what you're talking about…"

Ignoring him, I hurried and continued, "In fact, we have a recording of that phone conversation as well as text messages that we would love the court to hear. Ms. Drayson has also gone on record admitting your involvement in raping Janet, in an attempt to discredit Damien with a plan to get him kicked off his team and out of the league."

Facing the jury, I shared my next words with them.

"To shed some light, my client Mr. Roseland arrived at Ms. Springer's house for a planned party with Vincent James. After the party, my client spent a couple of intimate hours with his then girlfriend before leaving for D.C. After leaving, video footage shows that Vincent James never left the party that night. In fact, he hid in a closet and assaulted a sleeping Janet, once Damien was gone. My client, Mr. Roseland, did nothing but go home and …"

"Ok!" boomed, our new star witness. "I raped her, okay? I did it because Shannon swore she would have me killed if I didn't bring her the money or get Damien out! I owe other people money too, in back gambling debts, so there was no way I could give her the two million. Damien didn't deserve to be in the NBA, I did! I would have been better than him if not for my injury!"

With a smirk, I turned back to face Damien and the rest of the audience and saw nothing but shocked faces. I knew that my job was done. Moments later, Vince was led out of the courtroom and into prison.

Epilogue

(Maya)

For the next few weeks, reporters and the public hounded me with questions regarding Damien's case. It was overwhelming, but at the same time, I was flattered. Not only were celebrities contacting me left and right to handle their cases, but I had also risen quickly in status at the law firm. A spread was done on me in *Black Bosses* magazine, for their leading African-American women issue. In short, life was good. I was finally being known for my talents and not my last name. Damien and I were closer than ever, and my parents couldn't be more proud of me.

Through it all, Damien, the well-sought-after playboy, decided to hang with the one person who he felt had his back, besides me and his mom. It's true, Damien and Janet decided to try their relationship again, and were plastered across all magazines and television stations. We didn't realize until the verdict was read, but Janet was in the courtroom the day the judge dismissed all charges against Damien and ordered Vince to be handcuffed. The only bad thing that I wondered about through all of this, was why did I keep attracting the wrong type of men? First, the gay boyfriend, then chicken boy, and now I was sleeping with the enemy.

Parking my car into an empty spot in front of my favorite restaurant, Chez Pierre, I sat still for a few minutes before picking up the glossy *Sports* magazine that lay beside me in the seat. Damien's face graced the cover, with Ivey's story on him as the feature article. She'd done an excellent job incorporating his background, career, and the rape case. The story alone had people talking. Before, people labeled him as a hot head and bad boy, now he was a Humanitarian and a role model in the black community. With a smile, I set the publication down and hopped out the car, venturing toward the front of the restaurant to meet my parents. They wanted to have a celebratory dinner for me. Walking inside, the maître d' stand was empty and the hostess was nowhere to be found. After a few moments of waiting, I decided to just walk in.

"Surprise!" yelled the crowd of about fifty-to-sixty friends, family, and colleagues. The partners from my office were even there. In the corner, I'd even noticed Mrs. Roseland, Mrs. Oliver, and Mr. Sherman. In the opposite corner stood Taylor, Ivey, and surprisingly, Tinsley! I stood stunned, with my mouth gaped open until Damien ran up and swooped me into his arms, Janet trailing close behind him. "Sis this is for you!" he beamed. "For being so fucking amazing at what you do. I can't thank you enough, for everything."

"I can't believe you put all this together for me!" I squealed in excitement.

"I wish I could take credit, Maya, but it was all Corey's planning," he said with a mischievous eye.

"I hope you like it, Maya," came a voice from the left of me. Still stunned, I waited for Corey to continue. "I know you've been through a lot these last couple of months, but when you're up to it I would love to take you out and get to know you better."

Looking the attractive man who stood before me, up-and-down, I was reminded of the first day I'd met him on the train. The feelings I'd felt at the time rushed back, causing a slight flush to cover my cheeks. There was no way I was letting this man get away. For the first time in a long time, I felt desirable and secure. No words were spoken as Corey touched the small of my back and brought it closer to him in an embrace. There was no other place I wanted to be.

Made in the USA
Middletown, DE
16 June 2018